"ADRIAN MOLE, SUPERSTAR!

Mole-mania shows no signs of tapering off..."
Newsweek

"The trouble with trying to read passages from the Adrian Mole diaries aloud...is that you find yourself laughing so hard you can't go on. It's that kind of book..."
Kansas City Star

"As enduring and insightful an adolescent as Holden Caulfield, Tom Sawyer, or Huckleberry Finn...should make even the soberest reader laugh out loud."
Publishers Weekly

"Everything he says is funny, but it's the kid's deadly seriousness about the agonies of growing up that makes suffering along with him such a pleasure."
Chicago Tribune

Other Avon Books by
Sue Townsend

THE GROWING PAINS OF ADRIAN MOLE

THE
SECRET DIARY OF
ADRIAN MOLE,
AGED 13¾

SUE TOWNSEND

AVON
PUBLISHERS OF BARD, CAMELOT, DISCUS AND FLARE BOOKS

For Colin
and also for Sean, Dan, Vicki and Elizabeth
with love and thanks

AVON BOOKS
A division of
The Hearst Corporation
105 Madison Avenue
New York, New York 10016

First Avon Printing: September 1987
First Flare Printing: March 1984

AVON TRADEMARK REG. U.S. PAT. OFF. AND IN OTHER COUNTRIES,
MARCA REGISTRADA, HECHO EN U.S.A.

Printed in the U.S.A.

K-R   10   9   8   7   6   5   4

"Paul walked with something screwed up tight inside him . . . yet he chatted away with his mother. He would never have confessed to her how he suffered over these things and she only partly guessed."

D. H. Lawrence, *Sons and Lovers*

Thursday January 1st
BANK HOLIDAY IN ENGLAND,
IRELAND, SCOTLAND AND WALES

These are my New Year's resolutions:

1. I will help the blind across the road.
2. I will hang my trousers up.
3. I will put the sleeves back on my records.
4. I will not start smoking.
5. I will stop squeezing my spots.
6. I will be kind to the dog.
7. I will help the poor and ignorant.
8. After hearing the disgusting noises from downstairs last night, I have also vowed never to drink alcohol.

My father got the dog drunk on cherry brandy at the party last night. If the RSPCA hear about it he could get done. Eight days have gone by since Christmas Day but my mother still hasn't worn the green lurex apron I bought her for Christmas! She will get bathcubes next year.

Just my luck, I've got a spot on my chin for the first day of the New Year!

Friday January 2nd
BANK HOLIDAY IN SCOTLAND. FULL MOON

I felt rotten today. It's my mother's fault for singing "My Way" at two o'clock in the morning at the top of the stairs. Just my luck to have a mother like her. There is a chance my parents could be alcoholics. Next year I could be in a children's home.

The dog got its own back on my father. It jumped up and knocked down his model ship, then ran into the garden with the rigging tangled in its feet. My father kept saying, "Three months' work down the drain," over and over again.

The spot on my chin is getting bigger. It's my mother's fault for not knowing about vitamins.

Saturday January 3rd

I shall go mad through lack of sleep! My father has banned the dog from the house so it barked outside my window all night. Just my luck! My father shouted a swear-word at it. If he's not careful he will get done by the police for obscene language.

I think the spot is a boil. Just my luck to have it where everybody can see it. I pointed out to my mother that I hadn't had any vitamin C today. She said, "Go and buy an orange, then." This is typical.

She still hasn't worn the lurex apron.

I will be glad to get back to school.

Sunday January 4th
SECOND AFTER CHRISTMAS

My father has got the flu. I'm not surprised with the diet we get. My mother went out in the rain to get him a vitamin C drink, but as I told her, "It's too late now." It's a miracle we don't get scurvy. My mother says she can't see anything on my chin, but this is guilt because of the diet.

The dog has run off because my mother didn't close the gate. I have broken the arm on the stereo. Nobody knows yet, and with a bit of luck my father will be ill for a long time. He is the only one who uses it apart from me. No sign of the apron.

Monday January 5th

The dog hasn't come back yet. It is peaceful without it. My mother rang the police and gave a description of the dog. She made it sound worse than it actually is: straggly hair over its eyes and all that. I really think the police have got better things to do than look for dogs, such as catching murderers. I told my mother this but she still rang them. Serve her right if she was murdered because of the dog.

My father is still lazing about in bed. He is supposed to be ill, but I noticed he is still smoking!

Nigel came round today. He has got a tan from his Christmas holiday. I think Nigel will be ill soon from the shock of the cold in England. I think Nigel's parents were wrong to take him abroad.

He hasn't got a single spot yet.

Tuesday   January 6th
EPIPHANY. NEW MOON

The dog is in trouble!

It knocked a meter-reader off his bike and messed all the cards up. So now we will all end up in court I expect. A policeman said we must keep the dog under control and asked how long it had been lame. My mother said it wasn't lame, and examined it. There was a tiny model pirate trapped in its left front paw.

The dog was pleased when my mother took the pirate out and it jumped up the policeman's tunic with its muddy paws. My mother fetched a cloth from the kitchen but it had strawberry jam on it where I had wiped the knife, so the tunic was worse than ever. The policeman went then. I'm sure he swore. I could report him for that.

I will look up *Epiphany* in my new dictionary.

Wednesday   January 7th

Nigel came round on his new bike this morning. It has got a water bottle, a milometer, a speedometer, a yellow saddle, and very thin racing wheels. It's wasted on Nigel. He only goes to the shops and back on it. If I had it, I would go all over the country and have an experience.

My spot or boil has reached its peak. Surely it can't get any bigger!

I found a word in my dictionary that describes my father. It is *malingerer*. He is still in bed guzzling vitamin C.

The dog is locked in the coal shed.

Epiphany is something to do with the three wise men. Big deal!

Thursday   January 8th

Now my mother has got the flu. This means that I have to look after them both. Just my luck!

I have been up and down the stairs all day. I cooked a big dinner for them tonight: two poached eggs with beans, and tinned semolina pudding. (It's a good job I wore the green lurex apron because the poached eggs escaped out of the pan and got all over me.) I nearly said something when I saw they hadn't eaten *any* of it. They can't be that ill. I gave it to the dog in the coal shed. My grandmother is coming tomorrow morning, so I had to clean the burnt saucepans, then take the dog for a walk. It was half-past eleven before I got to bed. No wonder I am short for my age.

I have decided against medicine for a career.

Friday   January 9th

It was cough, cough, cough last night. If it wasn't one it was the other. You'd think they'd show some consideration after the hard day I'd had.

My grandma came and was disgusted with the state of the house. I showed her my room which is always neat and tidy and she gave me fifty pence. I showed her all the empty drink bottles in the dustbin and she was disgusted.

My grandma let the dog out of the coal shed. She said my mother was cruel to lock it up. The dog was sick on the kitchen floor. My grandma locked it up again.

She squeezed the spot on my chin. It has made it worse. I told grandma about the green apron and grandma said that she bought my mother a one hundred percent acrylic cardigan every Christmas and my mother had *never ever* worn one of them!

Saturday January 10th

A.M. Now the dog is ill! It keeps being sick so the vet has got to come. My father told me not to tell the vet that the dog had been locked in the coal shed for two days.

I have put a plaster over the spot to stop germs getting in it from the dog.

The vet has taken the dog away. He says he thinks it has got an obstruction and will need an emergency operation.

My grandma has had a row with my mother and gone home. My grandma found the Christmas cardigans all cut up in the duster bag. It is disgusting when people are starving.

Mr. Lucas from next door has been in to see my mother and father who are still in bed. He brought a "get well" card and some flowers for my mother. My mother sat up in bed in a nightie that showed a lot of her chest. She talked to Mr. Lucas in a yukky voice. My father pretended to be asleep.

Nigel brought his records round. He is into punk, but I don't see the point if you can't hear the words. Anyway I think I'm turning into an intellectual. It must be all the worry.

P.M. I went to see how the dog is. It has had its operation. The vet showed me a plastic bag with lots of yukky things in it. There was a lump of coal, the fir tree from the Christmas cake, and the model pirates from my father's ship. One of the pirates was waving a cutlass which must have been very painful for the dog. The dog looks a lot better. It can come home in two days, worse luck.

My father was having a row with my grandma on the phone about the empty bottles in the dustbin when I got home.

Mr. Lucas was upstairs talking to my mother. When Mr. Lucas went, my father went upstairs and had an argument with my mother and made her cry. My father is in a bad mood. This means he is feeling better. I made my mother a cup of tea without her asking. This made her cry as well. You can't please some people!

The spot is still there.

Sunday   January 11th
FIRST AFTER EPIPHANY

Now I *know* I am an intellectual. I saw Malcolm Muggeridge on the television last night, and I understood nearly every word. It all adds up. A bad home, poor diet, not liking punk. I think I will join the library and see what happens.

It is a pity there aren't any more intellectuals living round here. Mr. Lucas wears corduroy trousers, but he's an insurance man. Just my luck.

The first what after Epiphany?

Monday   January 12th

The dog is back. It keeps licking its stitches, so when I am eating I sit with my back to it.

My mother got up this morning to make the dog a bed to sleep in until it's better. It is made out of a cardboard box that used to contain packets of soap powder. My father said this would make the dog sneeze and burst its stitches, and the vet would charge even more to stitch it back up again. They had a row about the box, then my father went on about Mr. Lucas. Though what Mr. Lucas has to do with the dog's bed is a mystery to me.

Tuesday January 13th

My father has gone back to work. Thank God! I don't know how my mother sticks him.

Mr. Lucas came in this morning to see if my mother needed any help in the house. He is very kind. Mrs. Lucas was next door cleaning the outside windows. The ladder didn't look very safe. I have written to Malcolm Muggeridge, c/o the BBC, asking him what to do about being an intellectual. I hope he writes back soon because I'm getting fed up being one on my own. I have written a poem, and it only took me two minutes. Even the famous poets take longer than that. It is called "The Tap," but it isn't really about a tap, it's very deep, and about life and stuff like that.

The Tap, by Adrian Mole
The tap drips and keeps me awake,
In the morning there will be a lake.
For the want of a washer the carpet will spoil,
Then for another my father will toil.
My father could snuff it while he is at work.
Dad, fit a washer don't be a burk!

I showed it to my mother, but she laughed. She isn't very bright. She still hasn't washed my PE shorts, and it is school tomorrow. She is not like the mothers on television.

Wednesday January 14th

Joined the library. Got *Care of the Skin, Origin of Species,* and a book by a woman my mother is always going on about. It is called *Pride and Prejudice,* by a woman called Jane Austen. I could tell the librarian was impressed. Perhaps she is an intellectual like me. She didn't look at my spot, so perhaps it is getting smaller. About time!

Mr. Lucas was in the kitchen drinking coffee with my mother. The room was full of smoke. They were laughing, but when I went in, they stopped.

Mrs. Lucas was next door cleaning the drains. She looked as if she was in a bad mood. I think Mr. and Mrs. Lucas have got an unhappy marriage. Poor Mr. Lucas!

None of the teachers at school have noticed that I am intellectual. They will be sorry when I am famous. There is a new girl in our class. She sits next to me in Geography. She is all right. Her name is Pandora, but she likes being called "Box." Don't ask me why. I might fall in love with her. It's time I fell in love, after all I am 13¾ years old.

Thursday   January 15th

Pandora has got hair the color of treacle, and it's long like girls' hair should be. She has got quite a good figure. I saw her playing netball and her chest was wobbling. I felt a bit funny. I think this is it!

The dog has had its stitches out. It bit the vet, but I expect he's used to it. (The vet I mean; I know the dog is.)

My father found out about the arm on the stereo. I told a lie. I said the dog jumped up and broke it. My father said he will wait until the dog is completely cured of its operation then kick it. I hope this is a joke.

Mr. Lucas was in the kitchen again when I got home from school. My mother is better now, so why he keeps coming round is a mystery to me. Mrs. Lucas was planting trees in the dark. I read a bit of

Pride and Prejudice, but it was very old-fashioned. I think Jane Austen should write something a bit more modern.

The dog has got the same color eyes as Pandora. I only noticed because my mother cut the dog's hair. It looks worse than ever. Mr. Lucas and my mother were laughing at the dog's new haircut which is not very nice, because dogs can't answer back, just like the Royal Family.

I am going to bed early to think about Pandora and do my backstretching exercises. I haven't grown for two weeks. If this carries on I will be a midget.

I will go to the doctor's on Saturday if the spot is still there. I can't live like this with everybody staring.

Friday   January 16th

Mr. Lucas came round and offered to take my mother shopping in the car. They dropped me off at school. I was glad to get out of the car what with all the laughing and cigarette smoke. We saw Mrs. Lucas on the way. She was carrying big bags of shopping. My mother waved, but Mrs. Lucas couldn't wave back.

It was Geography today so I sat next to Pandora for a whole hour. She looks better every day. I told her about her eyes being the same as the dog's. She asked what kind of dog it was. I told her it was a mongrel.

I lent Pandora my blue felt-tip pen to color round the British Isles.

I think she appreciates these small attentions.

I started *Origin of Species* today, but it's not as good as the television series. *Care of the Skin* is dead good. I have left it open on the pages about vitamins. I hope my mother takes the hint. I have left it on the kitchen table near the ashtray, so she is bound to see it.

I have made an appointment about the spot. It has turned purple.

Saturday   January 17th

I was woken up early this morning. Mrs. Lucas is concreting the front of their house, and the concrete lorry had to keep its engine running while she shoveled the concrete round before it set. Mr. Lucas made her a cup of tea. He really is kind.

Nigel came round to see if I wanted to go to the pictures but I told him I couldn't, because I was going to the doctor's about the spot. He said he couldn't see a spot, but he was just being polite because the spot is massive today.

Dr. Taylor must be one of those overworked GPs you are always reading about. He didn't examine the spot, he just said I mustn't worry and was everything all right at home. I told him about my bad home life and my poor diet, but he said I was well nourished and to go home and count my blessings. So much for the National Health Service.

I will get a paperround and go private.

Sunday   January 18th
SECOND AFTER EPIPHANY. OXFORD HILARY TERM STARTS

Mrs. Lucas and my mother have had a row over the dog. Somehow it escaped from the house and trampled on Mrs. Lucas's wet concrete. My father offered to have the dog put down, but my mother started to cry so he said he wouldn't. All the neighbors were out in the street washing their cars and listening. Sometimes I really hate the dog!

I remembered my resolution about helping the poor and ignorant today, so I took some of my old *Beano* annuals to a quiet poor family who have moved into the next street. I know they are poor because they have only got a black and white telly. A boy answered the door. I explained why I had come. He looked at the annuals and said, "I've read 'em," and slammed the door in my face. So much for helping the poor!

Monday   January 19th

I have joined a group at school called the Good Samaritans. We go out into the community helping and stuff like that. We miss Math on Monday afternoons.

Today we had a talk on the sort of things we will be doing. I have been put in the old age pensioners' group. Nigel has got a dead yukky job looking after kids in a playgroup. He is as sick as a parrot.

I can't wait for next Monday. I will get a cassette so I can tape all the old fogies' stories about the war and stuff. I hope I get one with a good memory.

The dog is back at the vet's. It has got concrete stuck on its paws. No wonder it was making such a row on the stairs last night. Pandora smiled at me in school dinner today, but I was choking on a piece of gristle so I couldn't smile back. Just my luck!

Tuesday   January 20th
FULL MOON

My mother is looking for a job!

Now I could end up a delinquent roaming the streets and all that. And what will I do during the holidays? I expect I will have to sit in a launderette all day to keep warm. I will be a latchkey kid, whatever that is. And who will look after the dog? And what will I have to eat all day? I will be forced to eat crisps and sweets until my skin is ruined and my teeth fall out. I think my mother is being very selfish. She won't be any good in a job anyway. She isn't very bright and she drinks too much at Christmas.

I rang my grandma up and told her, and she says I could stay at her house in the holidays, and go to the Evergreens' meetings in the afternoons and stuff like that. I wish I hadn't rung now. The Samaritans met today during break. The old people were shared out. I got an old man called Bert Baxter. He is eighty-nine so I don't suppose I'll have him for long. I'm going round to see him tomorrow. I hope he hasn't got a dog. I'm fed up with dogs. They are either at the vet's or standing in front of the television.

Wednesday January 21st

Mr. and Mrs. Lucas are getting a divorce! They are the first down our road. My mother went next door to comfort Mr. Lucas. He must have been very upset because she was still there when my father came home from work. Mrs. Lucas has gone somewhere in a taxi. I think she has left forever because she has taken her socket set with her. Poor Mr. Lucas, now he will have to do his own washing and stuff.

My father cooked the tea tonight. We had boil-in-the-bag curry and rice, it was the only thing left in the freezer apart from a bag of green stuff which has lost its label. My father made a joke about sending it to the public health inspector. My mother didn't laugh. Perhaps she was thinking about poor Mr. Lucas left on his own.

I went to see old Mr. Baxter after tea. My father dropped me off on his way to play badminton. Mr. Baxter's house is hard to see from the road. It has got a massive overgrown privet hedge all round it. When I knocked on the door a dog started barking and growling and jumping up at the letterbox. I heard the sound of bottles being knocked over and a man swearing before I ran off. I hope I have got the wrong number.

I saw Nigel on the way home. He told me Pandora's father is a milkman! I have gone off her a bit.

Nobody was in when I got home so I fed the dog, looked at my spots and went to bed.

Thursday   January 22nd

It is a dirty lie about Pandora's father being a milkman! He is an accountant at the dairy. Pandora says she will duff Nigel up if he goes round committing libel. I am in love with her again.

Nigel has asked me to go to a disco at the youth club tomorrow night; it is being held to raise funds for a new packet of ping-pong balls. I don't know if I will go because Nigel is a punk on weekends. His mother lets him be one providing he wears a string vest under his bondage T-shirt.

My mother has got an interview for a job. She is practicing her typing and not doing any cooking. So what will it be like if she *gets* the job? My father should put his foot down before we are a broken home.

Friday   January 23rd

That is the last time I go to a disco. Everybody there was a punk except me and Rick Lemon, the youth leader. Nigel was showing off all night. He ended up putting a safety pin through his ear. My father had to take him to the hospital in our car. Nigel's parents haven't got a car because his father's got a steel plate in his head and his mother is only four feet eleven inches tall. It's not surprising Nigel has turned out bad really, with a maniac and a midget for parents.

I still haven't heard from Malcolm Muggeridge.

Perhaps he is in a bad mood. Intellectuals like him and me often have bad moods. Ordinary people don't understand us and say we are sulking, but we're not.

Pandora has been to see Nigel in hospital. He has got a bit of blood poisoning from the safety pin. Pandora thinks Nigel is dead brave. I think he is dead stupid.

I have had a headache all day because of my mother's rotten typing, but I'm not complaining. I must go to sleep now. I've got to go and see Bert Baxter tomorrow at his house. It was the right number WORSE LUCK!

Saturday January 24th

Today was the most terrible day of my life. My mother has got a job doing her rotten typing in an insurance office! She starts on Monday! Mr. Lucas works at the same place. He is going to give her a lift every day.

And my father is in a bad mood—he thinks his big-end is going.

But worst of all, Bert Baxter is not a nice old age pensioner! He drinks and smokes and has an alsatian dog called Sabre. Sabre was locked in the kitchen while I was cutting the massive hedge, but he didn't stop growling once.

But even worse than that! Pandora is going out with Nigel!!!!! I think I will never get over this shock.

Sunday January 25th
THIRD AFTER EPIPHANY

10 A.M. I am ill with all the worry, too weak to write much. Nobody has noticed I haven't eaten any breakfast.

2 P.M. Had two junior aspirins at midday and rallied a bit. Perhaps when I am famous and my diary is dis-

covered people will understand the torment of being
a 13¾-year-old undiscovered intellectual.
6 P.M. Pandora! My lost love!

Now I will never stroke your treacle hair! (Although my blue felt-tip is still at your disposal.)
8 P.M. Pandora! Pandora! Pandora!
10 P.M. Why? Why? Why?
Midnight. Had a crab-paste sandwich and a satsuma
(for the good of my skin). Feel a bit better. I hope
Nigel falls off his bike and is squashed flat by a lorry.
I will never speak to him again. He knew I was in
love with Pandora! If I'd had a racing bike for Christmas instead of a lousy digital stereo alarm clock,
none of this would have happened.

Monday   January 26th

I had to leave my sick-bed to visit Bert Baxter before
school. It took me ages to get there, what with feeling weak and having to stop for a rest every now and
again, but with the help of an old lady who had a
long black mustache I made it to the front door.
Bert Baxter was in bed but he threw the key down
and I let myself in. Sabre was locked in the bathroom; he was growling and sounded as if he was rip-
ping up towels or something.

Bert Baxter was lying in a filthy-looking bed
smoking a cigarette, there was a horrible smell in
the room, I think it came from Bert Baxter himself.
The bed sheets looked as though they were covered
in blood, but Bert said that was caused by the
beetroot sandwiches he always eats last thing at
night. It was the most disgusting room I have ever
seen (and I'm no stranger to squalor). Bert Baxter
gave me ten pence and asked me to get him the
Morning Star from the newsagent's. So he is a communist as well as everything else! Sabre usually

fetches the paper but he is being kept in as a punishment for chewing the sink.

The man in the newsagent's asked me to give Bert Baxter his bill (he owes for his papers £31.97), but when I did Bert Baxter said, "Smarmy four-eyed git," and laughed and ripped the bill up. I was late for school so I had to go to the school secretary's office and have my name put in the late book. That's the gratitude I get for being a Good Samaritan! I didn't miss Math either! Saw Pandora and Nigel standing close together in the dinner queue but chose to ignore them.

Mr. Lucas has taken to his bed because of being deserted so my mother is taking care of him when she finishes work. She is the only person he will see. So when will she find time to look after me and my father?

My father is sulking, I think he must be jealous because Mr. Lucas doesn't want to see *him*.

Midnight. Goodnight Pandora my treacle-haired love.

XXXXXXXXX

Tuesday   January 27th

Art was dead good today. I painted a lonely boy standing on a bridge. The boy had just lost his first love to his ex-best friend. The ex-best friend was struggling in the torrential river. The boy was watching his ex-best friend drown. The ex-best friend looked a bit like Nigel. The boy looked a bit like me. Ms. Fossington-Gore said my picture "had depth," so did the river. Ha! Ha! Ha!

Wednesday   January 28th

LAST QUARTER

I woke up with a bit of a cold this morning. I asked my mother for a note to excuse me from games. She said she refused to nambypamby me a day longer! How would she like to run about on a muddy field in the freezing drizzle, dressed only in PE shorts and a singlet? When I was in the school sports day three-legged race last year she came to watch me, *and* she had her fur coat on *and* she put a blanket round her legs, *and* it was only June! Anyway my mother is sorry now, we had rugger and my PE stuff was so full of mud that it has clogged up the drain hose on the washing machine.

The vet rang up to demand that we come and fetch the dog back from his surgery. It has been there nine days. My father says it will have to stay there until he gets paid tomorrow. The vet only takes cash and my father hasn't got any.

Pandora! Why?

Thursday   January 29th

The stupid dog is back. I am not taking it for a walk until its hair grows back on its shaved paws. My father looked pale when he came home from the vet's, he kept saying "It's money down the drain," and he said that from now on the dog can only be fed on leftovers from his plate.

This means the dog will soon starve.

Friday   January 30th

That filthy commie Bert Baxter has phoned the school to complain that I left the hedge-clippers out in the rain! He claims that they have gone all rusty. He wants compensation. I told Mr. Scruton, the headmaster, that they were already rusty but I could tell he didn't believe me. He gave me a lecture on how hard it was for old people to make ends meet. He has ordered me to go to Bert Baxter's and clean and sharpen the hedge-clippers. I wanted to tell the headmaster all about horrible Bert Baxter but there is something about Mr. Scruton that makes my mind go blank. I think it's the way his eyes pop out when he is in a temper.

On the way to Bert Baxter's I saw my mother and Mr. Lucas coming out of a betting shop together. I waved and shouted but I don't think they could have seen me. I'm glad Mr. Lucas is feeling better. Bert Baxter didn't answer the door. Perhaps he is dead.

Pandora! You are still on my mind, baby.

Saturday   January 31st

It is nearly February and I have got nobody to send a Valentine's Day card to.

Sunday   February 1st
FOURTH AFTER EPIPHANY

There was a lot of shouting downstairs late last night. The kitchen waste-bin was knocked over and the back door kept being slammed. I wish my parents would be a bit more thoughtful, I have been through an emotional time and I need my sleep. Still I don't expect them to understand what it is like being in love. They have been married for fourteen-and-a-half years.

Went to Bert Baxter's this afternoon but thank God he has gone to Skegness with the Evergreens. Sabre looked out of the living-room window. I gave him the "V" sign. I hope he doesn't remember.

Monday   February 2nd
PRESENTATION

Mrs. Lucas is back! I saw her pulling trees and bushes out of the earth and putting them in the back of a van, then she put all the gardening tools in and drove off. The van had "Women's Refuge" painted on the side. Mr. Lucas came over to our house to talk to my mother, I went down to say "hello" to him, but he was too upset to notice me. I asked my mother if she would get home early from work tonight, I'm fed up with waiting for my tea. She didn't.

Nigel got thrown out of school dinners today for swearing at the toad-in-the-hole, he said it was "all bleeding hole and no toad." I think Mrs. Leech was quite right to throw him out, after all the first-years were present! We third-years must set an example. Pandora has got up a petition to protest about the toad-in-the-hole. I will not sign it.

It was Good Samaritans today. So I was forced to go round to Bert Baxter's. I have missed the Algebra test! Ha! Ha! Ha! Bert gave me a stick of broken Skegness rock and said he was sorry he rang the school to complain about the hedge-clippers. He said he was lonely and wanted to hear a human voice. If I was the loneliest person in the world I wouldn't phone up our school. I would ring the speaking clock; that talks to you every ten seconds.

Tuesday   February 3rd

My mother has not done any proper housework for days now. All she does is go to work, comfort Mr. Lucas and read and smoke. The big-end has gone on my father's car. I had to show him where to catch a bus into town. A man of forty not knowing where the bus stop is! My father looked such a scruff-bag that I was ashamed to be seen with him. I was glad when the bus came. I shouted through the window that he couldn't sit downstairs and smoke but he just waved and lit up a cigarette. There is a fifty pounds' fine for doing that! If I was in charge of the buses I would fine smokers a thousand pounds *and* make them eat twenty Woodbines.

My mother is reading *The Female Eunuch,* by Germaine Greer. My mother says it is the sort of book that changes your life. It hasn't changed mine, but I only glanced through it. It is full of dirty words.

Wednesday   February 4th
NEW MOON

I had my first wet dream! So my mother was right about *The Female Eunuch*. It has changed my life.

The spot has got smaller.

Thursday   February 5th

My mother has bought some of those overalls that painters and decorators wear. You can see her knickers through them. I hope she doesn't wear them in the street.

She is having her ears pierced tomorrow. I think she is turning into a spendthrift. Nigel's mother is a spendthrift. They are always getting letters about having their electricity cut off and all because Nigel's mother buys a pair of high heels every week.

I would like to know where the Family Allowance goes, by rights it should be mine. I will ask my mother tomorrow.

Friday   February 6th
THE QUEEN'S ACCESSION, 1952

It is lousy having a working mother. She rushes in with big bags of shopping, cooks the tea then rushes around tarting herself up. But she is still not doing any tidying up before comforting Mr. Lucas. There has been a slice of bacon between the cooker and the fridge for three days to my knowledge!

I asked her about my Family Allowance today, she laughed and said she used it for buying gin and cigarettes. If the Social Services hear about it she will get done!

Saturday February 7th

My mother and father had been shouting at each other non-stop for hours. It started because of the bacon down the side of the fridge and carried on into how much my father's car is costing to repair. I went up to my room and put my Abba records on. My father had the nerve to crash my door open and ask me to turn the volume down. I did. When he got downstairs I turned it up again.

Nobody cooked any dinner so I went to the Chinese chip shop and bought a carton of chips and a sachet of soy sauce. I sat in the bus shelter and ate them, then walked about feeling sad. Came home. Fed dog. Read a bit of *Female Eunuch*. Felt a bit funny. Went to sleep.

Sunday February 8th
FIFTH AFTER EPIPHANY

My father came into my bedroom this morning, he said he wanted a chat. He looked at my Kevin Keegan scrapbook, screwed the knob of my wardrobe door back on with his Swiss army knife and asked me about school. Then he said he was sorry about yesterday and the shouting, he said my mother and him are "going through a bad patch." He asked me if I had anything to say. I said he owed me thirty-two pence for the Chinese chips and soy sauce. He gave me a pound. So I made a profit of sixty-eight pence.

Monday February 9th

There was a removal lorry outside Mr. Lucas's house this morning. Mrs. Lucas and some other women were carrying furniture from the house and stacking it on the pavement. Mr. Lucas was looking out from his bedroom window. He looked a bit frightened. Mrs.

Lucas was laughing and pointing up to Mr. Lucas and all the other women started laughing and singing "Why was he born so beautiful?"

My mother phoned Mr. Lucas up and asked him if he was all right. Mr. Lucas said he wasn't going to work today because he had to guard the stereo and records from his wife. My father helped Mrs. Lucas put the gas stove in the removal van, then he and my mother walked to the bus stop together. I walked behind them because my mother was wearing long dangly earrings and my father's trouser turn-ups had come down. They started to quarrel about something so I crossed over the road and went to school the long way round.

Bert Baxter was OK today. He told me about the First World War. He said his life was saved by a Bible he always carried in his breast pocket. He showed me the Bible, it was printed in 1956. I think Bert is going a bit senile.

Pandora! The memory of you is a constant torment!

Tuesday February 10th

Mr. Lucas is staying with us until he gets some new furniture.

My father has gone to Matlock to try to sell electric storage heaters to a big hotel.

Our gas boiler has packed in. It is freezing cold.

Wednesday February 11th
FIRST QUARTER

My father rang up from Matlock to say he has lost his Barclaycard and can't get home tonight, so Mr. Lucas and my mother were up all night trying to mend the boiler. I went down at ten o'clock to see if I could help but the kitchen door was jammed. Mr. Lucas said he couldn't open it just at that moment because he was at a crucial stage with the boiler and my mother was helping him and she had her hands full.

Thursday   February 12th
LINCOLN'S BIRTHDAY

I found my mother dyeing her hair in the bathroom tonight. This has come as a complete shock to me. For thirteen and three-quarter years I have thought I had a mother with red hair, now I find out that it is really light brown. My mother asked me not to tell my father. What a state their marriage must be in! I wonder if my father knows that she wears a padded bra? She doesn't hang them on the line to dry, but I have seen them shoved down the side of the airing cupboard. I wonder what other secrets my mother has got?

Friday   February 13th

It was an unlucky day for me all right!

Pandora doesn't sit next to me in Geography any more. Barry Kent does. He kept copying my work and blowing bubblegum in my ears. I told Miss Elf but she is scared of Barry Kent as well, so she didn't say anything to him.

Pandora looked luscious today, she was wearing a split skirt which showed her legs. She has got a scab on one of her knees. She was wearing Nigel's football scarf round her wrist, but Miss Elf saw it and told her to take it off. Miss Elf is not scared of Pandora. I have sent her a Valentine's Day card (Pandora, not Miss Elf).

Saturday February 14th
ST. VALENTINE'S DAY

I only got one Valentine's Day card. It was in my
mother's handwriting so it doesn't count. My
mother had a massive card delivered, it was so big
that a GPO van had to bring it to the door. She
went all red when she opened the envelope and
saw the card. It was dead good. There was a big
satin elephant holding a bunch of plastic flowers
in its trunk and a bubble coming out of its mouth
saying "Hi, Honey Bun! I ain't never gonna forget
you!" There was no name written inside, just
drawings of hearts with "Pauline" written inside
them. My father's card was very small and had a
bunch of purple flowers on the front. My father had
written on the inside "Let's try again."

Here is the poem I wrote inside Pandora's card.

Pandora!
I adore ya.
I implore ye
Don't ignore me.

I wrote it left-handed so that she wouldn't know it
was from me.

Sunday February 15th
SEPTUAGESIMA

Mr. Lucas moved back to his empty house last night.
I expect he got fed up with all the rowing over the elephant Valentine's Day card. I told my father that
my mother can't help it if a man secretly admires
her. My father gave a nasty laugh and said "You've
got a lot to learn, son."

I cleared off to my grandma's at dinner time. She
cooked me a proper Sunday dinner with gravy and

individual Yorkshire puddings. She is never too busy to make real custard either.

I took the dog with me and we all went for a walk in the afternoon to settle our dinners.

My grandma hasn't spoken to my mother since the row about the cardigans. Grandma says she "won't set foot in that house again!" Grandma asked me if I believed in life after death. I said I didn't and grandma told me that she had joined the Spiritualist church and has heard my grandad talking about his rhubarb. My grandad has been dead for four years!!! She is going on Wednesday night to try to get in touch with him again and she wants me to go with her. She says I have got an aura around me.

The dog choked on a chicken bone but we held it upside down and banged it hard, and the bone fell out. I've left the dog at grandma's to recover from its ordeal.

Looked up *Septuagesima* in my pocket dictionary. It didn't have it. Will look in the school dictionary, tomorrow.

Lay awake for ages thinking about God, Life and Death and Pandora.

Monday   February 16th
WASHINGTON'S BIRTHDAY OBSERVANCE

A letter from the BBC!!!!! A white oblong envelope with BBC in red fat letters. My name and address on the front! Could it be that they wanted my poems? Alas, no. But a letter from a bloke called John Tydeman, here is what he wrote:

Dear Adrian Mole,
Thank you for the poems which you sent to the BBC and which somehow landed up on my desk. I read them with interest and, taking into account your tender years, I must confess that they do

show some promise. However they are not of sufficient quality for us to consider including them in any of our current poetry programmes. Have you thought of offering them to your School Magazine or to your local Parish Magazine? (If you have one.)

If, in future, you wish to submit any of your work to the BBC may I suggest you get it typed out and retain, also, a copy for yourself. The BBC does not normally consider submissions in handwritten manuscript form and, despite the neatness of presentation, I did have some difficulty in making out *all* of the words — particularly at the end of one poem entitled "The Tap" where there was a rather nasty blotch which had caused the ink to run. (A teastain or a tearstain? A case of "Your Tap runneth over"!)

Since you wish to follow a literary career I suggest you will need to develop a thick skin in order to accept many of the inevitable future rejections you may receive with good grace and the minimum of personal pain.

With my best wishes to you for future literary efforts—and, above all, Good Luck!

Yours sincerely,
    John Tydeman

P.S. I enclose a poem by a certain John Mole which appeared in this week's *Times Literary Supplement.* Is he a relation? It is very good.

My mother and father were really impressed. I kept getting it out and reading it at school. I was hoping one of the teachers would ask to read it but none of them did.

Bert Baxter read it while I was doing his rotten washing up. He said they were "all a load of drug addicts in the BBC"! His brother-in-law's uncle once lived next door to a tea lady at Broadcasting House, so Bert knows all about the BBC.

Pandora got seventeen Valentine's Day cards. Nigel got seven. Even Barry Kent whom everybody hates got three! I just smiled when everybody asked me how many I got. Anyway I bet I am the only person in the school to get a letter from the BBC.

Tuesday February 17th

Barry Kent said he would "do me over" unless I gave him twenty-five pence every day. I told him that he was wasting his time demanding money with menaces from me. I never have any spare money. My mother puts my pocket money straight into my building-society account and gives me fifteen pence a day for a Mars bar. Barry Kent said I would have to give him my dinner money! I told him that my father pays it by check since it went up to fifty pence a day, but Barry Kent hit me in the goolies and walked off saying "There's more where that came from."

I have been to put my name down for a paper-round.

Wednesday February 18th
FULL MOON

Woke up with a pain in my goolies. Told my mother. She wanted to look but I didn't want her to so she said I would have to soldier on. She wouldn't give me a note excusing me from games, so I had to stumble around in the mud again. Barry Kent trod on my head in the scrum. Mr. Jones saw him and sent him off for an early shower.

I wish I could have a non-painful illness so I could be excused games. Something like a weak heart would be all right.

Fetched the dog from grandma's, she has given it a

shampoo and set. It smells like the perfume counter
in Woolworth's.

I went to the Spiritualist meeting with my
grandma, it was full of dead old people. One madman
stood up and said he had a radio inside his head
which told him what to do. Nobody took any notice of
him, so he sat down again. A woman called Alice
Tonks started grunting and rolling her eyes about
and talking to somebody called Arthur Mayfield, but
my grandad kept quiet. My grandma was a bit sad so
when we got home I made her a cup of Horlicks. She
gave me fifty pence and I walked home with the dog.

Started reading *Animal Farm,* by George Orwell. I
think I might like to be a vet when I grow up.

Thursday February 19th
PRINCE ANDREW BORN, 1960

It's all right for Prince Andrew, he is protected by
bodyguards. He doesn't have Barry Kent nicking
money off him. Fifty pence gone just like that! I wish
I knew karate, I would chop Barry Kent in his windpipe.

It is quiet at home, my parents are not speaking to
each other.

Friday February 20th

Barry Kent told Miss Elf to "get stuffed" in Geography today so she sent him to Mr. Scruton to be punished. I hope he gets fifty lashes. I am going to make
friends with Craig Thomas. He is one of the biggest
third-years. I bought him a Mars bar in break today.
I pretended I felt sick and didn't feel like eating it
myself. He said, "Ta Moley." That is the first time he
has spoken to me. If I play my cards right I could be
in his gang. Then Barry Kent wouldn't dare touch
me again.

My mother is reading another sex book, it is called

The Second Sex, by a frog writer called Simone De Beauvoir. She left it on the coffee table in the living room where anybody could have seen it, even my grandma!

Saturday February 21st

Had a dead good dream that Sabre was brutally savaging Barry Kent. Mr. Scruton and Miss Elf were watching. Pandora was there, she was wearing her split skirt. She put her arms round me and said, "I am of the second sex." Then I woke up to find I had had my second W.D. I have to put my pyjamas in the washing machine so my mother doesn't find out.

Had a good look at my face in the bathroom mirror today. I have got five spots as well as the one on my chin. I have got a few hairs on my lip. It looks as if I shall have to start shaving soon.

Went to the garage with my father, he expected to get the car back today but it still isn't ready. All the bits are on the work-bench. My father's eyes filled up with tears. I was ashamed of him. We walked to Sainsbury's. My father bought tins of salmon, crab and shrimps and a black forest cake and some dead yukky white cheese covered in grape pips. My mother was dead mad at him when we got home because he had forgotten the bread, butter and toilet paper. She says he can't be trusted to go on his own again. My father cheered up a bit.

Sunday February 22nd
SEXAGESIMA

My father has gone fishing with the dog. Mr. Lucas came for dinner and stayed for tea. He ate three slices of the black forest cake. We played Monopoly. Mr. Lucas was banker. My mother kept going into jail. I won because I was the only one concentrating properly. My father came in the front door and Mr.

Lucas went out of the back door. My father said he had been looking forward to the black forest cake all day. There was none left. My father said he had not had a bite to eat or a bite on his fishing line all day. My mother gave him grape-pip cheese on Ry-king for his supper. He threw it at the wall and said he wasn't a ******* mouse he was a ******* man and my mother said it was a long time since he had done any *******! I was sent out of the room then. It is a terrible thing to hear your own mother swearing. I blame it on all those books she has been reading. She hasn't ironed my school uniform yet, I hope she remembers.

I let the dog sleep in my room tonight, it doesn't like quarreling.

Monday February 23rd

Got a letter from Mr. Cherry the newsagent to say I can start a paperround tomorrow. Worse Luck!

Bert Baxter is worried about Sabre because he is off his food and not trying to bite anybody. He asked me to take him to the PDSA for a check-up. I said I would take him tomorrow if his condition hadn't improved.

I'm fed up with washing up for Bert. He seems to live off fried eggs, it is no joke trying to wash up in cold water without any washing-up liquid. Also there is never a dry tea towel. In fact there are never any tea towels and Sabre has ripped up all the bath towels so I don't know how Bert can even have a wash! I think I'll see if I can get Bert a home help.

I have got to concentrate on getting my GCEs if I want to be a vet.

Tuesday February 24th
ST. MATTHIAS

Got up at six o'clock for my paperround. I have got Elm Tree Avenue. It is dead posh. All the papers they read are very heavy: *The Times, The Daily Telegraph* and *The Guardian*. Just my luck!

Bert said Sabre is better, he tried to bite the milkman.

Wednesday   February 25th

Bed early tonight because of my paperround. Delivered twenty-five *Punches* as well as the papers.

Thursday   February 26th

The papers got mixed up today. Elm Tree Avenue got the *Sun* and the *Mirror* and Corporation Row got the heavy papers.

I don't know why everybody went so mad. You'd think they would enjoy reading a different paper for a change.

Friday   February 27th
LAST QUARTER

Early this morning I saw Pandora walking down the drive of 69 Elm Tree Avenue. She had a riding hat and jodhpurs on so she couldn't have been on her way to school. I didn't let her see me. I don't want her to know that I am doing a menial job.

So now I know where Pandora lives! I had a good look at the house. It is much bigger than ours. It has got rolled-up wooden blinds at all the windows, and the rooms look like jungles because of all the green plants. I looked through the letterbox and saw the big ginger cat eating something on the kitchen table. They have *The Guardian, Punch, Private Eye,* and *New Society*. Pandora reads *Jackie,* the comic for girls; she is not an intellecutal, like me. But I don't suppose Malcolm Muggeridge's wife is either.

Saturday February 28th

Pandora has got a little fat horse called "Blossom." She feeds it and makes it jump over barrels every morning before school. I know because I hid behind her father's Volvo and then followed her to a field next to the disused railway line. I hid behind a scrap car in the corner of the field and watched her. She looked dead good in her riding stuff, her chest was wobbling like mad. She will need to wear a bra soon. My heart was beating so loudly in my throat that I felt like a stereo loudspeaker, so I left before she heard me.

People complained because the papers were late. I had a *Guardian* left over in my paper bag so I took it home to read. It was full of spelling mistakes! It is disgusting when you think of how many people who can spell are out of work.

Sunday March 1st
QUINQUAGESIMA. ST. DAVID'S DAY

I took some sugar to Blossom before I did my paper-round. It brought me closer to Pandora somehow.

Have strained my back because of carrying all the Sunday supplements. Took the leftover *Sunday People* home as a present to my mother but she said it was only fit for lining the dustbin. Got my two pounds and six pence for six mornings, it is slave labor! *And* I have to give Barry Kent half of it. Mr. Cherry said he had a complaint from number 69 Elm Tree Avenue, that they didn't get a *Guardian* yesterday. Mr. Cherry sent a *Daily Express* round with his apologies, but Pandora's father brought it back to the shop and said he "would rather go without."

Didn't bother reading the papers today, I am fed up with papers. Had chow mein and beansprouts for Sunday dinner.

Mr. Lucas came round when my father had gone to visit grandma. He was wearing a plastic daffodil in his sports jacket.

My spots have completely gone. It must be early morning air.

Monday   March 2nd

My mother has just come into my room and said she had something awful to tell me. I sat up in bed and put a dead serious expression on my face just in case she'd got six months to live or she'd been caught shoplifting or something. She fiddled with the curtains, dropped cigarette ash all over my Concorde model and started mumbling on about "adult relationships" and "life being complicated" and how she must "find herself." She said she was fond of me. Fond!!! And would hate to hurt me. And then she said that for some women marriage was like being in prison. Then she went out.

Marriage is nothing like being in prison! Women are let out every day to go to the shops and stuff, and quite a lot go to work. I think my mother is being a bit melodramatic.

Finished *Animal Farm*. It is dead symbolic. I cried when Boxer was taken to the vet's. From now on I shall treat pigs with the contempt they deserve. I am boycotting pork of all kinds.

Tuesday   March 3rd
SHROVE TUESDAY

I gave Barry Kent his protection money today. I don't see how there can be a God. If there was, surely he wouldn't let people like Barry Kent walk about menacing intellectuals? Why are bigger youths unpleasant to smaller youths? Perhaps their brains are easily worn out with all the extra work they have to do making bigger bones and stuff, or it could be that the big youths have got brain damage because of all the sport they play, or perhaps big youths just *like* menacing and fighting. When I go to university I may study the problem.

I will have my thesis published and I will send a copy to Barry Kent. Perhaps by then he will have learnt to read.

My mother had forgotten that today was pancake day. I reminded her at 11 P.M. I'm sure she burnt them deliberately. I will be fourteen in one month's time.

Wednesday   March 4th
ASH WEDNESDAY

Had a nasty shock this morning. Took my empty paper sack back to Mr. Cherry's newsagent's and saw Mr. Lucas looking at those magazines on the top shelf. I stood behind the Mills and Boon rack and distinctly saw him choose *Big and Bouncy,* pay for it and leave the shop with it hidden inside his coat. *Big and Bouncy* is extremely indecent. It is full of disgusting pictures. My mother should be informed.

Thursday   March 5th

My father got his car back from the garage today. He was cleaning it and gloating over it for a whole two hours. I noticed that the stick-on waving hand I bought him for Christmas was missing from the rear window. I told him he ought to complain to the garage but he said he didn't want to make a fuss. We went to my grandma's to test-drive the car. She gave us a cup of Bovril and a piece of yukky seedcake. She didn't ask how my mother was, she said my father was looking thin and pale and needed "feeding up."

She told me that Bert Baxter had been thrown out of the Evergreens because of his bad behavior at Skegness. The coach was waiting for two hours for

him at the coach station. A search party was sent out
to look in the pubs, then Bert came back, drunk but
alone and another search party was sent out to look
for the first search party. In the end the police had to
be sent for and they took hours to round up all the
pensioners and get them in the coach.

My grandma said the journey back was a nightmare. All the pensioners kept falling out (with each
other not out of the coach). Bert Baxter was reciting
a dirty poem about an Eskimo and Mrs. Harriman
had a funny turn and had to have her corsets loos-
ened.

Grandma said two pensioners had passed on since
the outing, she blamed Bert Baxter and said "He as
good as murdered them," but I think it was more
likely that the cold wind at Skegness killed them off.
I said, "Bert Baxter is not so bad when you get to
know him." She said she didn't understand why the
Good Lord took my grandad and left scum like Baxter. Then she pulled her lips tight and dabbled her
eyes with a handkerchief, so we left.

My mother was out when we got home, she has
joined some woman's group.

Heard my father say "goodnight" to the car. He
must be cracking up!

Friday   March 6th
NEW MOON

Mr. Cherry is very pleased with my work and he has
raised my wages by two and a half pence an hour. He
also offered me the Corporation Row evening round,
but I declined his offer. Corporation Row is where
the council put all the bad tenants. Barry Kent lives
at number 13.

Mr. Cherry gave me two back copies of *Big and
Bouncy*. He told me not to tell my mother. As if I
would! I have put them under my mattress. Intellec-

tuals like me are allowed to be interested in sex. It is ordinary people like Mr. Lucas who should be ashamed of themselves.

Phoned Social Services today and asked about a home help for Bert Baxter. I told a lie and said I was his grandson. They are sending a social worker to see him on Monday.

Used my father's library tickets to get *War and Peace* out. I have lost my own.

Took dog to meet Blossom. They got on well.

Saturday March 7th

After paperround went back to bed and stayed there all morning reading *Big and Bouncy. Felt* like I have never *felt* before.

Went to Sainsbury's with my mother and father but the women in there reminded me of *Big and Bouncy,* even the ones over thirty! My mother said I looked hot and bothered and sent me back to the multi-storey car park to keep the dog company.

The dog already had company, it was barking and whining so loudly that a crowd of people were standing around saying "the poor thing" and "how cruel to leave it tied up in such a fashion." The dog had twisted its collar on the gear lever and its eyes were bulging out of its head. When it saw me it tried to jump up and nearly killed itself.

I tried to explain to the people that I was going to be a vet when I grew up, but they wouldn't listen and started to say things about the RSPCA. The car was locked so I was forced to break the little window open and unlock the door by putting my hand through. The dog went mad with joy when I untangled him, so the people went away. But my father didn't go mad with joy when he saw the damage, he went mad with rage. He threw the Sainsbury's bags down, broke the eggs, squashed the cakes and drove home too fast.

Nobody said anything on the way home, and only the dog was smiling.

Finished *War and Peace*. It was quite good.

Sunday   March 8th
FIRST IN LENT

My mother has gone to a woman's workshop on assertiveness training. Men aren't allowed. I asked my father what "assertiveness training" is. He said "God knows, but whatever it is, it's bad news for me."

We had boil-in-the-bag cod in butter sauce and oven-cooked chips for Sunday dinner, followed by tinned peaches and Dream-topping. My father opened a bottle of white wine and let me have some. I don't know much about wine but it seemed a pleasant enough vintage. We watched a film on television, then my mother came home and started bossing us around. She said, "The worm has turned," and "Things are going to be different around here," and things like that. Then she went into the kitchen and started making a chart dividing all the housework into three. I pointed out to her that I already had a paperround to do, an old age pensioner to look after and a dog to feed, as well as my school work, but she didn't listen, she put the chart on the wall and said "We start tomorrow."

Monday   March 9th
COMMONWEALTH DAY

Cleaned toilet, washed basin and bath before doing my paperround. Came home, made breakfast, put washing in machine, went to school. Gave Barry Kent his menaces money, went to Bert Baxter's, waited for social worker who didn't come, had school dinner. Had Domestic Science—made apple crumble. Came home. Vacuumed hall, lounge, and breakfast room. Peeled potatoes, chopped up cabbage, cut finger, rinsed blood off cabbage. Put chops under grill, looked in cookery book for a recipe for gravy. Made gravy. Strained lumps out with a colander. Set table, served dinner, washed up. Put burnt saucepans in to soak. Got washing out of machine; everything blue, including white underwear and handkerchiefs. Hung washing on clothes-horse. Fed dog. Ironed PE kit, cleaned shoes. Did homework. Took dog for a walk, had bath. Cleaned bath. Made three cups of tea. Washed cups up. Went to bed. Just my luck to have an assertive mother!

Tuesday   March 10th
PRINCE EDWARD BORN, 1964

Why couldn't I have been born Prince Edward and Prince Edward been born Adrian Mole? I am treated like a serf.

Wednesday   March 11th

Dragged myself to school after doing paperround and housework. My mother wouldn't give me a note excusing me from games so I left my PE kit at home. I just couldn't face running about in the cold wind.

That sadist Mr. Jones made me run all the way home to fetch my PE kit. The dog must have followed me out of the house because when I got to the school gate it was there before me. I tried to shut the dog out but it squeezed through the railings and followed me into the playground. I ran into the changing rooms and left the dog outside but I could hear its loud bark echoing around the school. I tried to sneak into the playing fields but the dog saw me and followed behind, then it saw the football and joined in the lesson! The dog is dead good at football, even Mr. Jones was laughing until the dog punctured the ball.

Mr. Scruton, the pop-eyed headmaster, saw everything from his window. He ordered me to take the dog home. I told him I would miss my sitting for school dinners but he said it would teach me not to bring pets to school.

Mrs. Leech, the kitchen supervisor, did a very kind thing. She put my curry and rice, spotted dick and custard into the oven to keep warm. Mrs. Leech doesn't like Mr. Scruton so she gave me a large marrow-bone to take home for the dog.

Thursday March 12th

Woke up this morning to find my face covered in huge red spots. My mother said they were caused by nerves but I am still convinced that my diet is inadequate. We had been eating a lot of boil-in-the-bag stuff lately. Perhaps I am allergic to plastic. My mother rang Dr. Gray's receptionist to make an appointment, but the earliest he can see me is next Monday! For all he knows I could have lassa fever and be spreading it all around the district! I told my mother to say that I was an emergency case but she said I was "overreacting as usual." She said a few spots didn't mean I was dying. I couldn't believe it when she said she was going to work as usual. Surely her child should come before her job?

I rang my grandma and she came round in a taxi and took me to her house and put me to bed. I am there now. It is very clean and peaceful. I am wearing my dead grandad's pyjamas. I have just had a bowl of barley and beef soup. It is my first proper nourishment for weeks.

I expect there will be a row when my mother comes home and finds that I have gone. But frankly, my dear diary, I don't give a damn.

Friday   March 13th
MOON'S FIRST QUARTER

The emergency doctor came to my grandma's last night at 11:30 P.M. He diagnosed that I am suffering from *acne vulgaris*. He said it was so common that it is regarded as a normal state of adolescence. He thought it was highly unlikely that I have got lassa fever because I have not been to Africa this year. He told grandma to take the disinfected sheets off the doors and windows. Grandma said she would like a second opinion. That was when the doctor lost his temper. He shouted in a very loud voice, "The lad has only got a few teenage spots, for Christ's sake!"

Grandma said she would complain to the Medical Council but the doctor just laughed and went downstairs and slammed the door. My father came round before he went to work and brought my Social Studies homework and the dog. He said that if I was not out of bed when he got home at lunchtime he would thrash me to within an inch of my life.

He took my grandma into the kitchen and had a loud talk with her. I heard him saying, "Things are very bad between me and Pauline, and all we are arguing over now is who *doesn't* get custody of Adrian." Surely my father made a mistake. He must have meant who *did* get custody of me.

So the worst has happened, my skin has gone to pot and my parents are splitting up.

Saturday   March 14th

It is official. They are getting a divorce! Neither of them wants to leave the house so the spare room is being turned into a bedsitter for my father. This could have a very bad effect on me. It could prevent me from being a vet.

My mother gave me five pounds this morning and

told me not to tell my father. I brought some bio-spot cream for my skin and the new Abba LP.

I rang Mr. Cherry and said I had personal problems and would be unable to work for a few weeks. Mr. Cherry said that he knew that my parents were divorcing because my father had canceled my mother's *Cosmopolitan.*

My father gave me five pounds and told me not to tell my mother. I spent some of it on buying some purple paper and envelopes so that the BBC will be impressed and read my poems. The rest of it will have to go on Barry Kent and his menaces money. I don't think anybody in the world can be as unhappy as me. If I didn't have my poetry I would be a raving loonie by now.

Went out for a sad walk and took Pandora's horse two pounds of cooking apples. Thought of a poem about Blossom. Wrote it down when I got back to the house where I live.

Blossom, by Adrian Mole, aged nearly fourteen

Little Brown Horse
Eating apples in a field,
Perhaps one day
My heart will be healed.
I stroke the places Pandora has sat
Wearing her jodhpurs and riding hat.
Goodbye, brown horse.
I turn and retreat,
The rain and mud are wetting my feet.

I have sent it to the BBC. I marked the envelope "Urgent."

Sunday March 15th
SECOND IN LENT

The house is very quiet. My father sits in the spare room smoking and my mother sits in the bedroom smoking. They are not eating much.

Mr. Lucas has phoned my mother three times. All she says to him is "not yet, it's too early." Perhaps he has asked her to go to the pub for a drink and take her mind off her troubles.

My father has put the stereo in his bedroom. He is playing his Jim Reeves records and staring out of the window. I took him a cup of tea and he said "Thanks, son" in a choked-up voice.

My mother was looking at old letters in my father's handwriting when I took her tea in; she said, "Adrian, what must you think of us?" I said that Rick Lemon, the youth leader, thinks divorce is society's fault. My mother said, "Bugger society."

I washed and ironed my school uniform ready for school tomorrow. I am getting quite good at housework.

My spots are so horrific that I can't bear to write about them. I will be the laughingstock at school.

I am reading *The Man in the Iron Mask*. I know exactly how he feels.

Monday March 16th

Went to school. Found it closed. In my anguish I had forgotten that I am on holiday. Didn't want to go home, so went to see Bert Baxter instead. He said the social worker had been to see him and had promised to get Sabre a new kennel but he can't have a home help. (Bert, not Sabre.)

There must have been a full week's washing-up in the sink again. Bert says he saves it for me because I make a good job of it. While I washed up I told Bert about my parents getting a divorce. He said he didn't hold with divorce. He said he was married for thirty-five miserable years so why should anybody else get away with it? He told me that he had got four children and that none of them come to see him. Two of them are in Australia so they can't be blamed, but I think the other two should be ashamed of themselves. Bert showed me a photograph of his dead wife, it was taken in the days before they had plastic surgery. Bert told me that he was a hostler when he got married (a hostler is somebody doing things with horses) and didn't really notice that his wife looked like a horse until he left to work on the railways. I asked him if he would like to see a horse again. He said he would, so I took him to see Blossom.

It took us ages to get there. Bert walks dead slow and he kept having to sit down on garden walls, but we got there eventually. Bert said that Blossom was not a horse, she was a girl pony. He kept patting her and saying "who's a beauty then, eh?" Then Blossom went for a run about so we sat down on the scrap car, and Bert had a Woodbine and I had a Mars bar. Then we walked back to Bert's house. I went to the shops and bought a packet of Vesta chow mein and a butterscotch Instant Whip for our dinner, so Bert ate a decent meal for once. We watched *Pebble Mill at One*, then Bert showed me his old horse brushes and photographs of the big house where he worked when he was a boy. He said he was made into a communist when he was there, but he fell asleep before he could tell me why.

Came home, nobody was in so I played my Abba records at the highest volume until the deaf woman next door banged on the wall.

Tuesday March 17th
ST PATRICK'S DAY. BANK HOLIDAY IN N. IRELAND AND
REP. OF IRELAND

Looked at *Big and Bouncy*. Measured my "thing." It
was eleven centimetres.

Mr. O'Leary who lives across the road from us was
drunk at ten o'clock in the morning! He got thrown
out of the butcher's for singing.

Wednesday March 18th

My mother and father are both speaking to solici-
tors. I expect they are fighting over who gets custody
of me. I will be a tug-of-love child, and my picture
will be in the newspapers. I hope my spots clear up
before then.

Thursday March 19th

Mr. Lucas has put his house up for sale. My mother
says the asking price is thirty thousand pounds!!

What will he do with all that money?

My mother says he will buy another bigger house.
How stupid can you get?

If I had thirty thousand pounds I would wander
the world having experiences.

I wouldn't take any real money with me because I
have read that most foreigners are thieves. Instead I
would have three thousand pounds' worth of travel-
ler's checks sewn into my trousers. Before I set off, I
would:

a) Send Pandora three dozen red roses.
b) Pay a mercenary fifty pounds to duff Barry
   Kent up.
c) Buy the best racing bike in the world and ride it
   past Nigel's house.

d) Order a massive crate of expensive dog food so that the dog is properly fed while I'm away.
e) Buy a housekeeper for Bert Baxter.
f) Offer my mother and father a thousand pounds *(each)* to stay together.

When I came back from the world I would be tall, brown and full of ironical experiences and Pandora would cry into her pillow at night because of the chance she missed to be Mrs. Pandora Mole. I would qualify to be a vet in record time then I would buy a farmhouse. I would convert one room into a study so that I could have somewhere quiet to be intellectual in.

I wouldn't waste thirty thousand pounds on buying a semi-detached house!

Friday   March 20th
FIRST DAY OF SPRING. FULL MOON

It is the first day of spring. The council have chopped all the elms down in Elm Tree Avenue.

Saturday   March 21st

My parents are eating different things at different times, so I usually have six meals a day because I don't want to hurt anyone's feelings.

The television is in my room now because they couldn't decide who it belongs to. I can lie in bed and watch the late-night horror.

I am starting to get a bit suspicious about my mother's feelings towards Mr. Lucas. I found a note she had from him; it says: "Pauline how much longer? For God's sake come away with me. Yours forever, Bimbo."

Although it was signed "Bimbo" I know it was from Mr. Lucas because it was written on the back of his red electricity bill.

My father should be informed. I have put the note under my mattress next to the *Big and Bouncy* magazines.

Sunday   March 22nd
THIRD IN LENT. BRITISH SUMMER TIME BEGINS

It is my grandma's birthday today; she is seventy-six and looks it. I took her a card and a pot plant; it is called Leopard Lily, its foreign name is *Dieffenbachia*. It had a plastic label stuck in the soil which said, "The sap in this plant is poisonous so take care." My grandma asked me who chose the plant. I told her my mother did.

My grandma is quite pleased that my parents are getting a divorce! She said that she always thought that my mother had a wanton streak in her and that now she had been proved right.

I didn't like to hear my mother being spoken of in such a way so I came home. I pretended to grandma that I had promised to meet a friend. But I haven't really got a friend any more, it must be because I'm an intellectual. I expect people are in awe of me. Looked in my dictionary to find out what *wanton* means. It is not very nice!

Monday   March 23rd

Back to school, worse luck! We had Domestic Science today. We did baked potatoes in the oven with cheese filling. My potatoes were bigger than anyone else's so they weren't properly cooked by the time the lesson ended, so I finished them off at Bert Baxter's. He wanted to see Blossom again which was a bit of a drag because he takes so long to walk anywhere. But we went, anything is better than doing Math at school.

Bert took his horse brushes with him and gave Blossom a good clean, she was shining like a conker by the time he'd finished. Bert got out of breath so he sat on the scrap car and had a Woodbine, then we walked back to Bert's house.

Sabre is in a better temper since he got his new kennel and Bert's house is in a better condition as a result of Sabre being outside. Bert told me that the social worker thought he ought to go into an old people's home where he can be properly looked after. Bert doesn't want to. He told a lie to the social worker, he said his grandson came in every day and looked after him. The social worker is going to check up so I could be in trouble for impersonation!!! I don't know how much more worry I can take.

Tuesday March 24th

Late last night I saw my mother and Mr. Lucas going out in Mr. Lucas's car. They went somewhere special because my mother was wearing a boiler suit with sequins. She did look a bit wanton. Mr Lucas was wearing his best suit and he had a lot of gold jewelery on. For an old person he certainly knows how to dress.

If my father took more care of his appearance, none of this would have happened. It stands to reason that any woman would prefer a man to wear a suit and a lot of gold jewelry to one like my father who hardly ever shaves and wears old clothes and no jewelery.

I am going to stay awake and find out what time my mother comes home.
Midnight. Mother still not home.
2 A.M. No sign of my mother.

Wednesday March 25th
ANNUNCIATION OF B.V. MARY

Fell asleep, so don't know what time my mother got home. My father said she had gone to the insurance firm's Christmas dinner and dance. In March! Come off it, dad! I was not born yesterday! We had swimming in Games today. The water was freezing cold and so were the changing cubicles. I will try to get athlete's foot so that I don't have to go next week.

Thursday   March 26th

Barry Kent has been done by the police for riding a bike without a rear light. I hope he gets sent to a Detention Center. A short sharp shock will do him good.

Friday   March 27th

Pandora and Nigel have split up! It is all round the school. This is the best news I have had for ages.

I am reading *Madame Bovary,* by another frog writer.

Saturday   March 28th
LAST QUARTER

Nigel has just left, he is heartbroken. I tried to comfort him. I said that there are plenty more pebbles on the beach and fish in the sea. But he was much too upset to listen.

I told him about my suspicions about my mother and Mr. Lucas and he said that it had been going on for a long while. Everybody knew except me and my father!!

We had a long talk about racing bikes, then Nigel went home to think about Pandora.

It is Mother's Day tomorrow. I am in two minds about whether to buy her something or not. I have only got sixty-eight pence.

Sunday   March 29th
FOURTH IN LENT. MOTHERING SUNDAY

My father gave me three pounds last night. He said,
"Get your mother something decent, son, it could be
the last time." I certainly wasn't going all the way
into town for her, so I went to Mr. Cherry's and
bought a box of Black Magic, and a card saying "To a
wonderful mother."

Card manufacturers must think that all mothers
are wonderful because every single card has "wonderful" written on it somewhere. I felt like crossing
"wonderful" out and putting "wanton" in its place,
but I didn't. I signed it "from your son, Adrian." I
gave it to her this morning. She said, "Adrian, you
shouldn't have." She was right, I shouldn't have.

Must stop now. My mother has arranged what she
called "a civilized meeting." Mr. Lucas is going to be
there. Naturally *I* am not invited! I am going to listen at the door.

Monday   March 30th

A terrible thing happened last night. My father and
Mr. Lucas had a fight in the *front* garden, the whole
street came outside to watch! My mother tried to separate them but they both told her to "keep out of it."
Mr. O'Leary tried to help my father, he kept shouting
"Give the smarmy bugger one for me, George." Mrs.
O'Leary was shouting horrible things at my mother.
By the sounds of things she had been watching my
mother's movements since Christmas. The civilized
meeting broke up at about five o'clock when my father found out how long my mother and Mr. Lucas
had been in love.

They had another civilized meeting at about seven
o'clock, but when my mother disclosed that she was
leaving for Sheffield with Mr. Lucas my father be-

came uncivilized and started fighting. Mr. Lucas ran into the garden but my father rugby-tackled him by the laurel bush and the fight broke out again. It was quite exciting really. I had a good view from my bedroom window. Mrs. O'Leary said, " 'Tis the child I feel sorry for," and all the people looked up and saw me, so I looked especially sad. I expect the experience will give me a trauma at some stage in the future. I'm all right at the moment, but you never know.

Tuesday   March 31st

My mother has gone to Sheffield with Mr. Lucas. She had to drive because Mr. Lucas couldn't see out of his black eyes. I have informed the school secretary of my mother's desertion. She was very kind and gave me a form to give my father; it is for free school dinners. We are now a single-parent family.

Nigel has asked Barry Kent to stop menacing me for a few weeks. Barry Kent said he would think about it.

Wednesday   April 1st
ALL FOOLS' DAY

Nigel rang up this morning and pretended he was an undertaker and asked when he was to pick up the body. My father answered the phone. Honestly! He has got no sense of humor.

I had a good laugh telling girls that their petticoats were showing when they weren't. Barry Kent brought a packet of itching powder into the Art lesson, he put some down Ms. Fossington-Gore's flying boots. She is another one without any sense of humor. Barry Kent put some down my back. It wasn't funny. I had to go to the matron and have it removed.

The house is looking extremely squalid because my father is not doing any housework. The dog is pining for my mother.

I was born exactly thirteen years and three hundred and sixty-four days ago.

Thursday   April 2nd

I am fourteen today! Got a track suit and a football from my father. (He is completely insensitive to my needs.) *A Boy's Book of Carpentry* from my grandma Mole. (No comment.) One pound inside a card from my grandad Sugden. (Last of the big spenders.) Best of all was ten pounds from my mother and five pounds from Mr. Lucas. (Conscience money.)

Nigel sent a joke card; it said on the front, "Who's sexy, charming intelligent and handsome?" Inside it said, "Well it certainly ain't you buddy!!!" Nigel wrote "No offense, mate." He put ten pence inside the envelope.

Bert Baxter sent a card to the school because he doesn't know where I live. His handwriting is dead good, I think it is called "brass plate." His card had a picture of an alsatian on the front. Inside Bert had written, "Best wishes from Bert and Sabre. P.S.

Drain blocked up." Inside the card there was a book token for ten shillings. It expired in December 1958, but it was a kind thought.

So at last I am fourteen! Had a good look at myself in the mirror tonight and I think I can detect a certain maturity. (Apart from the rotten spots.)

Friday April 3rd

Got full marks in the Geography test today. Yes! I am proud to report that I got twenty out of twenty! I was also complimented on the neat presentation of my work. There is nothing I don't know about the Norwegian leather industry. Barry Kent seems to take delight in being ignorant. When Miss Elf asked him where Norway was in relation to Britain he said, "First cousin twice removed." It hurts me to relate that even Pandora laughed with the rest of the class. Only Miss Elf and I remained composed. Unblocked Bert Baxter's drain, it was full of old bones and tea leaves. I told Bert that he really ought to use tea-bags. After all this is the twentieth century! Bert said that he would give them a try. I told him that my mother has run away with an insurance man, he said "Was it an Act of God?" Then he laughed until his eyes watered.

Saturday April 4th
NEW MOON

Me and my father cleaned the house up today. We had no choice: my grandma is coming for tea tomorrow. We went to Sainsbury's in the afternoon. My father chose a trolley that was impossible to steer. It also squeaked as if somebody was torturing mice. I was ashamed to be heard with it. My father chose food that is bad for you. I had to put my foot down and insist that he bought some fresh fruit and salad. When we got to the check-out he couldn't find his banker's card, the cashier wouldn't take a check without it, so the supervisor had to come and stop the argument. I had to lend my father some of my birthday money. So he owes me eight pounds thirty-eight and a half pence. I made him write an IOU on the back of the till roll.

But I must say that I take my hat off to Sainsbury's, they seem to attract a better class of person. I saw a vicar choosing toilet paper; he chose a four-roll pack of purple three-ply. He must have money to burn! He could have bought some shiny white and given the difference to the poor. What a hypocrite!

Sunday   April 5th
PASSION SUNDAY

Nigel came round this morning. He is still mad about Pandora. I tried to take his mind off her by talking about the Norwegian leather industry but he couldn't get interested somehow.

I made my father get up at 1 P.M. I don't see why he should lie stinking in bed all day when I am up and about. He got up and went outside to clean the car. He found one of my mother's earrings down the side of the back seat and he just sat there staring at it. He said, "Adrian, do you miss your mother?" I replied, "Of course I do, but life must go on." He then said, "I don't see why." I took this to mean that he was suicidal, so I immediately went upstairs and removed anything harmful from the bathroom.

After we had eaten our frozen roast-beef dinner and I was washing up, he shouted from the bathroom for his razor. I lied and shouted back that I didn't know where it was. I then removed every knife and sharp instrument from the kitchen drawer. He tried to get his battery razor to work but the batteries had leaked and gone all green.

I like to think I am broad-minded but the language

my father used was beyond the pale, and all because he couldn't have a shave! Tea was a bit of a drag. My grandma kept saying horrible things about my mother and my father kept rambling on about how much he missed her. Nobody even noticed I was in the room! The dog got more attention than me!

My grandma told my father off for growing a beard. She said, "You may think it amusing to look like a communist, George, but I don't." She said that even in the trenches at Ypres my grandad had shaved every day. Sometimes he had to stop rats from eating his shaving soap. She said that my grandad was even shaved by the undertaker when lying in his coffin, so if the dead could shave there was no excuse for the living. My father tried to explain, but grandma didn't stop talking once so it was a bit difficult.

We were both glad when she went home.

Looked at *Big and Bouncy*. It is Passion Sunday after all!

Monday   April 6th

Had a postcard from my mother. It said "they" were staying with friends until they found a flat. She said I could go and stay for a weekend when they were fixed up.

I didn't show it to my father.

Tuesday April 7th

My precious Pandora is going out with Craig Thomas. That's the last time you get a Mars bar from me, Thomas!

Barry Kent is in trouble for drawing a nude woman in Art. Ms. Fossington-Gore said that it wasn't so much the subject matter but his ignorance of basic biological facts that was so upsetting. I did a good drawing of the Incredible Hulk smashing Craig

Thomas to bits. Ms. Fossington-Gore said it was a "powerful statement of monolithic oppression."

Phone call from my mother. Her voice sounded funny as if she had a cold. She kept saying, "You'll understand one day, Adrian." There was a slurping sound in the background. I expect it was that Lucas creep kissing her neck. I have seen them do it on the films.

Wednesday April 8th

My father wouldn't give me a note excusing me from Games so I spent nearly all morning dressed in pyjamas diving into a swimming pool and picking up a brick from the bottom. I had a bath when I came home but I still smell of chlorine. I just don't see the point of the above lesson. When I am grown up I am hardly going to walk along a river bank in my pyjamas, am I? And who would be stupid enough to dive into a river for a boring old brick? Bricks are lying around all over the place!

Thursday April 9th

My father and me had a good talk last night. He asked me who I would prefer to live with, him or my mother? I said both. He told me he has made friends with a woman at work, she is called Doreen Slater. He said he would like me to meet her one day. Here we go again; so much for the suicidal, heartbroken, deserted husband!

Friday April 10th

Rang my grandmother to tell her about Doreen Slater. My grandma didn't sound too pleased, she said it was a common-sounding name and I am inclined to agree with her.

Got *Waiting for Godot* out of the library. Disap-

pointed to find that it was a play. Still, I will give it a
go. I have been neglecting my brain lately.

Nigel asked me if I wanted to stay the weekend.
His parents are going to a wedding in Croydon. My
father said I could. He looked quite pleased. I am
going round to Nigel's in the morning.

I broke up for the Easter holidays today. Must
make sure my brain keeps active.

Saturday　April 11th
FIRST QUARTER

Nigel is dead lucky. His house is absolutely fantastic! Everything is modern. I don't know what he
must think of our house, some of our furniture is
over a hundred years old!

His bedroom is massive and he has got a stereo, a
color televison, a tapedeck, a Scalextric track, an
electric guitar and amplifier. Spotlights over his bed.
Black walls and a white carpet and a racing car con-
tinental quilt. He has got loads of back issues of *Big
and Bouncy,* so we looked through them, then Nigel
had a cold shower while I cooked the soup and cut the
french loaf. We had a good laugh at *Waiting for
Godot.* Nigel had hysterics when I said that Vladi-
mir and Estragon sounded like contraception pills.

I had a go on Nigel's racing bike. I now want one
more than anything in the world. If I had to choose
between Pandora and a racing bike, I would choose
the bike. Sorry, Pandora, but that's how things are.

We went to the chip shop and had the works. Fish,
chips, pickled onions, gherkins, sloppy peas. Nothing
was too expensive for Nigel, he gets loads of pocket
money. We walked round for a bit, then we came back
and watched *The Bug Eyed Monster Strikes Back* on
the television. I said the bug-eyed monster reminded
me of Mr. Scruton the headmaster. Nigel had hysterics again. I think I have got quite a talent to amuse

people. I might change my mind about becoming a vet and try writing situation comedy for television.

When the film finished Nigel said, "How about a nightcap?" He went to the bar in the corner of the lounge and he poured us both a stiff whisky and soda. I hadn't actually tasted whisky before and I never will again. How people can drink it for pleasure I don't know. If it was in a medicine bottle they would pour it down the sink!

Don't remember going to bed, but I must have done because I am sitting up in Nigel's parents' bed writing my diary.

Sunday April 12th
PALM SUNDAY

This weekend with Nigel has really opened my eyes! Without knowing it I have been living in poverty for the past fourteen years. I have had to put up with inferior accommodation, lousy food and paltry pocket money. If my father can't provide a decent standard of living for me on his present salary, then he will just have to start looking for another job. He is always complaining about having to flog electric storage heaters anyway. Nigel's father has worked like a slave to create a modern environment for *his* family. Perhaps if *my* father had built a formica cocktail bar in the corner of *our* lounge my mother would still be living with us. But oh no. My father actually boasts about our hundred-year-old furniture.

Yes! Instead of being ashamed of our antiques, he is proud of the clapped-out old rubbish.

My father should take lessons from Great Literature. Madame Bovary ran away from that idiot Doctor Bovary because he couldn't supply her needs.

Monday April 13th

Had a note from Mr. Cherry asking me when I can resume my paperround. I sent a note back to say that due to my mother's desertion I am still in a mental state. This is true. I wore odd socks yesterday without knowing it. One was red and one was green. I must pull myself together. I could end up in a lunatic asylum.

Tuesday April 14th

Had a postcard from my mother. She has found a flat and she wants me to visit her and Lucas as soon as possible.

Why can't my mother write a letter like any normal person? Why should the postman be able to read my confidential business? Her new address is 79A, President Carter Walk, Sheffield.

I asked my father if I could go; he said, "Yes, providing she sends the train fare." So I have written a letter asking her to send eleven pounds eighty.

Wednesday April 15th

Went to the youth club with Nigel. It was dead good. We played ping-pong until the balls cracked. Then we had a go on the football table. I beat Nigel fifty goals to thirteen. Nigel went into a sulk and said that he only lost because his goalkeeper's legs were stuck on with Sellotape but he was wrong. It was my superior skill that did it.

A gang of punks passed unkind comments about my flared trousers but Rick Lemon, the youth leader, stepped in and led a discussion on personal taste. We all agreed it should be up to the individual to dress how he or she likes. All the same I think I will ask my father if I can have a new pair of trousers. Not many fourteen-years-olds wear flared trousers today, and I don't wish to be conspicuous.

Barry Kent tried to get in the fire-doors to avoid paying his five-pence subs. But Rick Lemon pushed him back outside into the rain. I was very pleased. I owe Barry Kent two pounds' menace money.

Thursday   April 16th

Got a birthday card from my Auntie Susan, two weeks late! She always forgets the right day. My father said that she's under a lot of pressure because of her job, but I can't see it myself. I'd have thought that being a prison wardress was dead cushy, it is only locking and unlocking doors after all. She has sent a present via the GPO so with luck I should get it by Christmas. Ha! Ha!

Friday   April 17th
GOOD FRIDAY

Poor Jesus, it must have been dead awful for him. I wouldn't have had the guts to do it myself.

The dog has mauled the hot-cross buns; it doesn't respect any traditions.

Saturday   April 18th

Got parcel from Auntie Susan. It is an embroidered toothbrush holder and it was made by one of the prisoners! She is called Grace Pool. Auntie Susan said that I should write and thank her! It is bad enough that my father's sister works in Holloway Prison. But now I am expected to start writing to the prisoners! Grace Pool could be a murderess or anything!

Still waiting for the eleven pounds eighty pence. It doesn't seem as if my mother is desperate to see me.

Sunday April 19th
EASTER SUNDAY

Today is the day that Jesus escaped from the cave. I expect that Houdini got the idea from him.

My father forgot to go to the bank on Friday so we are penniless. I had to take the pop bottles back to the shop to buy myself an Easter egg. Watched film, then had a fantastic tea at grandma's. She made a cake covered in little fluffy chicks. Some of the fluff got into my father's mouth, he had to have his back thumped hard. He always manages to spoil things. He has got no Social Decorum at all. Went to see Bert Baxter after tea. He was pleased to see me and I felt a bit rotten because I have neglected him lately. He gave me a pile of comics. They are called the *Eagle* and they have got great pictures. I read them until 3 A.M. this morning. Us intellectuals keep anti-social hours. It does us good.

Monday April 20th
BANK HOLIDAY IN UK (EXCEPT SCOTLAND)

My father is in a rage because the bank is still shut. He has run out of cigarettes. It will do him good. No sign of the eleven pounds eighty pence.

Wrote to Grace Pool. She is in 'D' Wing. I put:

Dear Miss Pool,
Thank you for making the toothbrush holder. It is charming.

    Yours, with kind regards, Adrian

Tuesday April 21st

My father was first in the queue at the bank this morning. When he got inside the cashier said he couldn't have any money because he hadn't got any left. My father demanded to see the manager. I was dead ashamed so I sat behind a plastic plant and waited until the shouting had stopped. Mr Niggard, the head bloke, came out and calmed my father down. He said he would arrange a temporary overdraft. My father looked dead pathetic, he kept saying, "It was that bloody vet's bill." Mr. Niggard looked as if he understood. Perhaps he has got a mad dog as well. We can't be the only ones, can we?

The eleven pounds, etc., came by second post so I am going to Sheffield tomorrow morning. I've never been on a train on my own before. I am certainly stretching my wings lately.

Wednesday   April 22nd

My father gave me a lift to the station. He also gave me a bit of advice about the journey; he said I was not to buy a pork pie from the buffet car.

I stood in the train with my head out of the window and my father stood on the platform. He kept looking at his watch. I couldn't think of anything to say and neither could he. In the end I said, "Don't forget to feed the dog, will you?" My father gave a nasty laugh, then the train started to move so I waved and went to look for a non-smoking seat. All the filthy smokers were crammed together choking and coughing. They were a rough-looking, noisy lot so I hurried through their small carriage holding my breath. The non-smoking carriages seemed to have a quieter type of person in them. I found a window seat opposite an old lady. I had wanted to look at the landscape or read my book but the old bat started on about her daughter's hysterectomy and telling me things I didn't want to hear. She just about sent me barmy! It was nag, nag, nag. But thank God she got off at Chesterfield. She left her *Woman's Own* behind so I had a good laugh at the Problem Page, read the story, and then the train slowed down for Sheffield. My mother started crying when she saw me. It was a bit embarrassing but quite nice at the same time. We got a taxi from the station, Sheffield looks OK, just like home really. I didn't see any knife and fork factories. I expect Margaret Thatcher has closed them all down.

Lucas was out flogging insurance so I had my mother all to myself until eight o'clock. The flat is dead grotty, it is modern but small. You can hear the neighbors coughing. My mother is used to better things. I am dead tired, so will stop.

I hope my father is being kind to the dog. I wish my mother would come home, I had forgotten how nice she is.

Thursday   April 23rd
ST. GEORGE'S DAY

Me and mum went shopping today. We bought a Habitat lampshade for her bedroom and a new pair of trousers for me. They are dead good, really tight.

We had a Chinese Businessman's Lunch and then went to see a Monty Python film all about the life of Jesus. It was dead daring, I felt guilty laughing.

Lucas was at the flat when we got back. He had got the dinner ready but I said I wasn't hungry and I went to my room. It would choke me to eat anything that creep had touched! Later on I phoned my father from a call-box; I just had time to shout, "Don't forget to feed the dog," before the pips went.

Retired to bed early because of all the slopping Lucas was doing. He calls my mother "Paulie" when he knows very well that her name is Pauline.

Friday April 24th

Helped my mother to paint her kitchen. She is doing it brown and cream, it looks awful, just like the toilets at school. Lucas bought me a penknife. He is trying to bribe me into liking him again. Hard luck, Lucas! Us Moles never forget. We are just like the Mafia, once you cross us we bear a grudge all our lives. He has stolen a wife and mother so he will have to pay the price! It is a shame because the penknife is full of gadgets that would be useful to me in my everyday life.

Saturday April 25th

Lucas doesn't work on Saturdays so I had to put up with his lechery all day. He is constantly touching my mother's hand or kissing her or putting his arm around her shoulders, I don't know how she stands it, it would drive me mad.

Lucas drove us out into the countryside this afternoon, it was hilly and high up. I got cold so I sat in the car and watched my mother and Lucas making an exhibition of themselves. Thank God, no members of the public were around. It is not a pretty sight to see old people running up hills laughing.

Came back, had a bath, thought about the dog, went to sleep.

Home tomorrow.

3 A.M. Just had a dream about stabbing Lucas with the toothpick on my penknife. Best dream I've had for ages.

Sunday April 26th

2:10 P.M. So my little sojourn in Sheffield is drawing to a close. I am catching the 7.10 P.M. train which only leaves five hours to do my packing. My father was right. I didn't need two suitcases of clothes. Still it is better to be safe than sorry, I always say. I shan't be sorry to leave this sordid flat with the coughing neighbors, though naturally I have some regrets about my mother's stubbornness in refusing to come home with me.

I told her that the dog was pining to death for her but she rang my father up and like a fool he told her that the dog had just eaten a whole tin of Pedigree Chum and a bowl of Winalot.

I told her about my father and Doreen Slater, hoping to send her mad with jealousy, but she just laughed and said, "Oh, is Doreen still making the rounds?" I have done my best to get her back, but must admit defeat.

11 P.M. Journey back a nightmare, non-smoking compartments all full, forced to share carriage with pipes, cigars and cigarettes. Queued for twenty minutes for a cup of coffee in the buffet. Just got to the counter when the grill came down and the man put up a sign saying: "Closed due to signal failure"! Got back to seat, found a soldier in my place. Found another seat, but had to endure maniac sitting opposite telling me he had a radio inside his head controlled by Fidel Castro.

My father met me at the station, the dog jumped up to meet me, missed, and nearly fell in front of the 9:23 P.M. Birmingham express.

My father said he had had Doreen Slater for tea. By the state of the house I should think he'd had her for breakfast, dinner and tea! I have never seen the woman, but from the evidence she left behind I know she has got bright red hair, wears orange lipstick and sleeps on the left side of the bed.

What a homecoming!

My father said Doreen had ironed my school clothes ready for the morning. What did he expect? Thanks?

Monday   April 27th

Mrs. Bull taught us to wash up in Domestic Science.
Talk about teaching your grandmother to suck eggs!
I must be one of the best washer-uppers in the world!
Barry Kent broke an unbreakable plate so Mrs. Bull
sent him out of the room. I saw him smoking quite
openly in the corridor. He has certainly got a nerve! I
felt it was my duty to report him to Mrs. Bull. I did
this purely out of concern for Barry Kent's health.
He was taken to pop-eye Scruton and his *Benson and
Hedges* were confiscated. Nigel said he saw Mr.
Scruton smoking them in the staff room at dinner-
time, but surely this can't be true?

   Pandora and Craig Thomas are creating a scandal
by flaunting their sexuality in the playground. Miss
Elf had to knock on the staffroom window and ask
them to stop kissing.

Tuesday   April 28th

Mr. Scruton made a speech in assembly this morning.
It was about the country's lack of morals, but really
he was talking about Pandora and Craig Thomas.
The speech didn't do any good because while we were
singing "There is a Green Hill Far Away," I distinctly
saw glances of a passionate nature pass between
them.

Wednesday   April 29th

My father is worried, electric storage heaters are not
selling well. My father says this proves that consum-
ers are not as stupid as everyone thinks. I'm fed up
with him mooning about the house at night. I have
advised him to join a club or get a hobby but he is determined to feel sorry for himself. The only time he
laughs is when those advertisements for electric

storage heaters are shown on televison. Then he laughs himself silly.

Thursday   April 30th

I was seriously menaced at school today. Barry Kent threw my snaplock executive brief-case on to the rugby pitch. I have got to find two pounds quickly before he starts throwing *me* on to the rugby pitch. It's no good asking my father for money, he is in despair because of all the red bills.

Friday   May 1st

Grandma rang early this morning to say "Cast ne'er a clout till May be out." I haven't got the faintest idea what she was going on about. All I know is that it has something to do with vests.

I am pleased to report that Barry Kent and his gang have been banned from the "off the streets" youth club. (But this means that they are now *on* the streets, worse luck.) They filled a French letter with water and threw it at a bunch of girls and made them scream. Pandora burst the thing with a badge pin and Rick Lemon came out of his office and slipped in the water. Rick was dead mad, he got dirty marks all over his yellow trousers. Pandora helped Rick to throw the gang out, she looked dead fierce. I expect she will win the medal for "Most helpful member of the year."

Saturday   May 2nd

Had a letter from Grace Pool! This is what it said:

Dear Adrian,
Thank you for your charming letter of thanks. It fair brightened up my day. The girls are all joshing me about my suitor. I am due for parole on

June 15th, would it be possible to come and see you? Your Auntie Susan is one of the best screws in here, that's why I obliged and made the tooth-brush holder. See you on the fifteenth then.

Yours with fond regards,
Grace Pool

P.S. I was falsely convicted of arson but that is all in the past now.

My God! What shall I do?

Sunday May 3rd
SECOND AFTER EASTER

There is nothing left in the freezer, nothing in the pantry and only slimming bread in the bread bin. I don't know what my father does with all the money. I was forced to go round to grandma's before I died from malnutrition. At four o'clock I had one of those rare moments of happiness that I will remember all my life. I was sitting in front of grandma's electric coal fire eating dripping toast and reading the *News of the World*. There was a good play on Radio Four about torturing in concentration camps. Grandma was asleep and the dog was being quiet. All at once I felt this dead good feeling. Perhaps I am turning religious.

I think I have got it in me to be a Saint of some kind.

Phoned Auntie Susan but she is on duty in Hollo-way. Left a message with her friend Gloria, asking Auntie Susan to ring me urgently.

Monday May 4th
BANK HOLIDAY IN UK. NEW MOON

Auntie Susan rang to say that Grace Pool has had her parole canceled because she set fire to the embroidery workshop and destroyed a gross of tooth-brush holders.

Their loss is my gain!

Tuesday May 5th

Saw our postman on the way to school, he said that my mother is coming to visit me on Saturday. I've a good mind to report him to the Postmaster General for reading a person's private postcard!

My father had also read my postcard by the time I got home from school. He looked pleased and started cleaning rubbish out of the lounge, then he rang Doreen Slater and said he would have to "take a rain check on Saturday's flick." Grown-ups are always telling adolescents to speak clearly then they go and talk a lot of gibberish themselves. Doreen Slater shouted down the phone. My father shouted back that he "didn't want a long-term relationship," he had "made that clear from the start," and that "nobody could replace his Pauline." Doreen Slater went shrieking on and on until my father slammed the phone down. The phone kept ringing until my father took the phone off the hook. He went mad doing housework until 2 A.M. this morning, and it's only Tuesday! What will he be like on Saturday morning? The poor fool is convinced that my mother is coming back for good.

Wednesday May 6th

I am proud to report that I have been made a school-dinner monitor. My duties are to stand at the side of the pig bin and make sure that my fellow pupils scrape their plates properly.

Thursday   May 7th

Bert Baxter rang the school to ask me to call round urgently. Mr. Scruton told me off, he said the school telephone was not for the convenience of the pupils. Get stuffed, Scruton, you pop-eyed git!!! Bert was in a terrible state. He has lost his false teeth. He has had them since 1946, they have got sentimental value for him because they used to belong to his father. I looked everywhere for them, but couldn't find them.

I went to the shops and brought him a tin of soup and a butterscotch Instant Whip. It was all he could manage at the moment. I have promised to go round tomorrow and look again. Sabre was happy for once; he was chewing something in his kennel.

My father is still cleaning the house up. Even Nigel commented on how clean the kitchen floor looked. I wish my father wouldn't wear the apron though, he looks like a poofter in it.

Friday   May 8th

Found Bert's teeth in Sabre's kennel. Bert rinsed them under the tap and put them back in his mouth! This is the most revolting thing I have ever seen.

My father has got bunches of flowers to welcome my mother home. They are all over the house stinking the place out.

Mr. Lucas's house has been sold at last. I saw the estate agent's minion putting the board up. I hope the new people are respectable. I am reading the *Mill on the Floss,* by a bloke called George Eliot.

Saturday   May 9th

I was woken up at 8:30 by a loud banging on the front door. It was an Electricity Board official. I was amazed to hear that he had come to turn off our electricity! My father owes £95.79p. I told the official that we need electricity for life's essentials like the television and stereo, but he said that people like us are sapping the country's strength. He went to the meter cupboard, did something with tools, and the second hand on the kitchen clock stopped. It was dead symbolic. My father came in from fetching the *Daily Express*. He was whistling and looking dead cheerful. He even asked the official if he would like a cup of tea! The official said, "No thank you," and hurried up the path and got into his little blue van. My father switched the electric kettle on. I was forced to tell him.

Naturally I got the blame! My father said I should have refused entry. I told him that he should have put all the bill money away each week like grandma does. But he just went berserk. My mother turned up with Lucas! It was just like old times with everybody shouting at once. I took the dog to the shops and bought five boxes of candles. Mr. Lucas lent me the money.

When I got back I stood in the hall and heard my mother say, "No wonder you can't pay the bills, George; just look at all these flowers. They must have cost a fortune." She said it very kindly. Mr. Lucas said he would lend my father a "ton" but my father was very dignified and said, "All I want from you, Lucas, is my wife." My mother complimented my father on how nicely he was keeping the house. My father just looked sad and old. I felt dead sorry for him.

I was sent outside while they talked about who was getting custody of me, the arguing went on for ages. In fact until it was time to light the candles.

Lucas spilt candle-wax over his new suede shoes. It was the only cheerful incident in a tragic day.

When my mother and Lucas had gone off in a taxi I went to bed with the dog. I heard my father talking to Doreen Slater on the phone, then the front door slammed and I looked out of my window to see him driving off in the car. The back seat was full of flowers.

Sunday May 10th
THIRD AFTER EASTER. MOTHER'S DAY, USA AND CANADA. MOON'S FIRST QUARTER

Didn't get up until half-past four this afternoon. I think I am suffering from depression. Nothing happened at all today, apart from a hail storm around six o'clock.

Monday May 11th

Bert Baxter offered to lend us a paraffin heater. Our gas central heating won't work without electricity. I thanked him but refused his kind offer. I have read that they are easily knocked over and our dog would no doubt cause a towering inferno.

If it gets out that our electricity has been cut off, I will cut my throat. The shame would be too much to bear.

Tuesday May 12th

Had a long talk with Mr. Vann the Career teacher today. He said that if I want to be a vet I will have to do Physics, Chemistry and Biology for O level. He said that Art, Woodwork and Domestic Science won't do much good.

I am at the Crossroads in my life. The wrong decision now could result in a tragic loss to the veterinary world. I am hopeless at science. I asked Mr. Vann which O levels you need to write situation comedy for television. Mr. Vann said that you don't need qualifications at all, you just need to be a moron.

Wednesday May 13th

Had an in-depth talk about O levels with my father, he advised me to only do the subjects that I am good at. He said that vets spend half their working life with their hands up cows' bums, and the other half injecting spoiled fat dogs. So I am rethinking my future career prospects.

I wouldn't mind being a sponge-diver, but I don't think there is much call for them in England.

Thursday May 14th

Miss Sproxton told me off because my English essay was covered in drops of candle-wax. I explained that I had caught my overcoat sleeve on the candle whilst doing my homework. Her eyes filled with tears and she said I was "a dear brave lad," and she gave me a merit mark.

After supper of cream crackers and tuna fish, played cards in the candlelight. It was dead good. My father cut the ends off our gloves, we looked like two criminals on the run.

I am reading *Hard Times*, by Charles Dickens.

Friday May 15th

My grandma has just made a surprise visit. She caught us huddled round our new Camping-gaz stove eating cold beans out of a tin. My father was reading *Playboy* under cover of the candlelight and I was reading *Hard Times* by my key-ring torch. We were quite contented. My father had just said that it was a "good training for when civilization collapses" when grandma burst in and started having hysterics. She has forced us to go to her house so I am there now sleeping in my dead grandad's bed. My father is sleeping downstairs on two armchairs pushed together. Grandma has written a Giro check for the electricity money, she is furious because she wanted the money for restocking her freezer. She buys two dead cows a year.

Saturday May 16th

Helped grandma with the weekend shopping. She was dead fierce in the grocer's; she watched the scales like a hawk watching a fieldmouse. Then she pounced and accused the shop assistant of giving her underweight bacon. The shop assistant was dead scared of her and put another slice on.

Our arms were dead tired by the time we'd staggered up the hill carrying big bags of shopping. I don't know how my grandma does it when she's alone. I think the council ought to put escalators on hills; they would save money in the long run, old people wouldn't go about collapsing all over the place. My father paid the electricity bill at the post office today, but it will be at least a week before the computer gives permission for our electricity to be reconnected.

Sunday May 17th

My grandma made us get up early and go to church with her. My father was made to comb his hair and wear one of his dead father's ties. Grandma held both our arms and looked proud to be with us. The church service was dead boring. The vicar looked like the oldest man alive and spoke in a feeble sort of voice. My father kept standing up when we were supposed to sit down and vice versa. I copied what grandma did, she was always right. My father sang too loudly, everyone looked at him. I shook the vicar's hand when we were allowed outside. It was like touching dead leaves.

After dinner we listened to my grandma's records

of Al Jolson, then grandma went upstairs for a sleep and my father and me washed up. My father broke a forty-one-year-old milk jug! He had to go out for a drink to recover from the shock. I went to see Bert Baxter but he wasn't in, so I went to see Blossom instead. She was very pleased to see me. It must be dead boring standing in a field all day long. No wonder she welcomes visitors.

Monday   May 18th

Grandma is not speaking to my father because of the milk jug. Can't wait to get home where things like milk jugs don't matter.

Tuesday   May 19th
FULL MOON

My father is in trouble for staying out late last night. Honestly! He is the same age as the milk jug so surely he can come in what time he likes!

Told my father about being menaced today. I was forced to because Barry Kent seriously damaged my school blazer and tore the school badge off. My father is going to speak to Barry Kent tomorrow *and* he is going to get all the menaces money back off him, so it looks like I could be rich!

Wednesday   May 20th

Barry Kent denied all knowledge of menacing me and laughed when my father asked him to repay the money. My father went to see his father and had a serious argument and threatened to call the police. I think my father is dead brave. Barry Kent's father looks like a big ape and has got more hair on the back of his hands than my father has got on his entire head.

The police have said that they can't do anything

without proof so I am going to ask Nigel to give them a sworn statement that he has seen me handing menaces money over.

Thursday   May 21st

Barry Kent duffed me up in the cloakroom today. He hung me on one of the coathooks. He called me a "coppers' nark" and other things too bad to write down. My grandma found out about the menacing (my father didn't want her to know on account of her diabetes). She listened to it all then she put her hat on, thinned her lips and went out. She was gone one hour and seven minutes, she came in, took her coat off, fluffed her hair out, took £27.18 from the antimugger belt round her waist. She said, "He won't bother you again, Adrian, but if he does, let me know." Then she got the tea ready. Pilchards, tomatoes and ginger cake. I bought her a box of diabetic chocolates from the chemist's as a token of my esteem.

Friday   May 22nd

It is all round the school that an old lady of seventy-six frightened Barry Kent and his dad into returning my menaces money. Barry Kent daren't show his face. His gang are electing a new leader.

Saturday   May 23rd

Home again, the electricity has been reconnected. All the plants are dead. Red bills on the doormat.

Sunday   May 24th
ROGATION SUNDAY

I have decided to paint my room black; it is a color I like. I can't live a moment longer with Noddy wallpaper. At my age it is positively indecent to wake up to Big Ears and all the rest of the Toyland idiots running around the walls. My father says I can use any color I like so long as I buy the paint and do it myself.

Monday   May 25th

I have decided to be a poet. My father said that there isn't a suitable career structure for poets and no pensions and other boring things, but I am quite decided. He tried to interest me in becoming a computer operator, but I said, "I need to put my soul into my work and it is well known that computers haven't got a soul." My father said, "The Americans are working on it." But I can't wait that long.

Bought two tins of black vinyl silk-finish paint and a half-inch brush. Started painting as soon as I got home from the DIY center. Noddy keeps showing through the black paint. Looks like it'll need two coats. Just my luck!

Tuesday   May 26th
MOON'S LAST QUARTER

Now put on two coats of black paint! Noddy still showing through! Black paw-marks over landing and stairs. Can't get paint off hands. Hairs falling out of brush. Fed up with whole thing. Room looks dark and gloomy. Father hasn't lifted a finger to help. Black paint everywhere.

Wednesday   May 27th

Third coat. Slight improvement, only Noddy's hat showing through now.

Thursday   May 28th
ASCENSION DAY

Went over Noddy's hat with kid's paintbrush and
last of black paint, but bloody hat bells are still
showing through!

Friday   May 29th

Went over hat bells with black felt-tip pen, did
sixty-nine tonight, only a hundred and twenty-four
to go.

Saturday   May 30th

Finished last bell at 11:25 P.M. Know just how
Rembrandt must have felt after painting the Sistine
Chapel in Venice.
2 A.M. The paint is dry but it must have been faulty
because it is all streaky, and here and there you can
see Gollywog's striped trousers and Mr. Plod's nose.
Thank God the bloody bells don't show through! My
father has just been in to tell me to go to sleep, he
said my room reminded him of a Salvador Dali painting. He said it was a surrealist nightmare, but he is
only jealous because he has got yukky roses on his
bedroom walls.

Sunday   May 31st
SUNDAY AFTER ASCENSION

I bought a joss stick from Mr. Singh's shop. I lit it in
my room to try and get rid of the paint smell. My father came into my room and threw the joss stick out
of the window, he said he "wouldn't have me messing
with drugs"! I tried to explain but my father was too
angry to listen. I stayed in my room for a few hours
but the black walls seemed to be closing in on me so I
went to see Bert Baxter. Couldn't make him hear, so
I came home and watched religion on the television.

Had tea, did Geography homework, went to bed. Dog won't stay in room any more; it whimpers to be let out.

Monday June 1st
BANK HOLIDAY IN THE REP. OF IRELAND

My father had a letter that made his face go white: he has been made redundant from his job! He will be on the dole! How can we live on the pittance that the government will give us? The dog will have to go! It costs thirty-five pence a day for dog food, not counting Winalot. I am now a single-parent child whose father is on the dole! Social Security will be buying my shoes!

I didn't go to school today, I rang the school secretary and told her that my father is mentally ill and needs looking after. She sounded dead worried and asked if he was violent. I said that he hadn't shown any signs of being violent, but if he started I would call the doctor. I made my father lots of hot, sweet drinks for shock, he kept going on about electric storage heaters and saying that he would spill the beans to the media.

He rang Doreen Slater up and she came round straightaway, she had a horrible little kid called Maxwell with her. It was quite a shock to see Doreen Slater for the first time. Why my father wanted to have carnal knowledge of her I can't imagine. She is as thin as a stick insect. She has got no bust and no bum.

She is just straight all the way up and down, including her nose and mouth and hair. She put her arms round my father as soon as she came into the house. Maxwell started to cry, the dog started to bark, so I went back to my black room and counted how many things were now showing through the paint: a hundred and seventeen!

Doreen left at 1:30 P.M. to take Maxwell to play-school. She did some shopping for us then cooked a sloppy sort of meal made of spaghetti and cheese. She is a one-parent family; Maxwell was born out of wedlock. She told me about herself when we were washing up. She would be quite nice if she were a bit fatter.

Tuesday   June 2nd
NEW MOON

Doreen and Maxwell stayed the night. Maxwell was supposed to sleep on the sofa, but he cried so much that he ended up sleeping in the double bed between my father and Doreen, so my father was unable to extend his carnal knowledge of Doreen. He was as sick as a pig, but not as sick as Maxwell was. Ha! Ha! Ha!

Wednesday   June 3rd

Went to school today, couldn't concentrate, kept thinking about the stick insect. She has got lovely white teeth (straight of course). She made some jam tarts for when I came home from school. She is not stingy with the jam like some women are.

My father is smoking and drinking heavily, but he has been made temporarily impotent according to Doreen. This is something I do not wish to know! Doreen talks to me as if I were another adult instead of her lover's son aged fourteen and two months and one day.

Thursday   June 4th

Doreen answered the phone to my mother first thing this morning. My mother asked to speak to me. She demanded to know what Doreen was doing in the house. I told her that my father was having a breakdown and that Doreen Slater was looking after him. I told her about his redundancy. I said he was drinking heavily, smoking too much and generally letting himself go. Then I went to school. I was feeling rebellious, so I wore red socks. It is strictly forbidden but I don't care any more.

Friday   June 5th

Miss Sproxton spotted my red socks in assembly! The old bag reported me to pop-eyed Scruton. He had me in his office and gave me a lecture on the dangers of being a nonconformist. Then he sent me home to change into regulation black socks. My father was in bed when I got home; he was having his impotence cured. I watched *Play School* with Maxwell until he came downstairs. I told him about the sock saga.

He instantly turned into a raving loonie! He phoned the school and dragged Scruton out of a caretakers' strike-meeting. He kept shouting down the phone; he said, "My wife's left me, I've been made redundant, I'm in charge of an idiot boy," — Maxwell, I presume — "and you're victimizing my son because of the color of his socks!" Scruton said if I came to school in black socks everything would be forgotten but my father said I would wear whatever color socks I liked. Scruton said he was anxious to maintain standards. My father said that the England World Cup team in 1966 did not wear black socks, nor did Sir Edmund Hillary in 1953. Scruton seemed to go quiet then. My father put the phone down. He said, "Round one to me."

This could well get into the papers: "Black socks row at school." My mother might read about it and come home.

Saturday June 6th

Oh Joy! Oh Rapture! Pandora is organizing a sock protest! She came round to my house today! Yes! She actually stood on our front porch and told me that she admired the stand I was taking! I would have asked her in, but the house is in a squalid state so I didn't. She is going round the school with a petition on Monday morning. She said I was a freedom fighter for the rights of the individual. She wants me to go round her house tomorrow morning. A committee is being set up, and I am the principal speaker! She wanted to see the red socks but I told her they were in the wash.

Doreen Slater and Maxwell went home today. My grandma is coming round tonight, so all traces of them have got to be wiped out.

Sunday June 7th
WHIT SUNDAY

Grandma found Maxwell's dummy in my father's bed. I lied and said that the dog must have brought it in off the street. It was a nasty moment. I am not a good liar, my face goes bright red and my grandma has got eyes like Superman's, they seem to bore right through you. To divert her I told her about the red-sock row, but she said rules were made to be kept.

Pandora and the committee were waiting for me in the big lounge of her house. Pandora is Chairperson, Nigel is Secretary and Pandora's friend Claire Neilson is Treasurer. Craig Thomas and his brother Brett are just ordinary supporters. I am not allowed to hold high office because I am the victim.

Pandora's parents were in the wooden kitchen doing *The Sunday Times* crossword. They seem to get on quite well together.

They brought a tray of coffee and health biscuits into the lounge for us. Pandora introduced me to her parents. They said they admired the stand that I was taking. They are both members of the Labor Party and they went on about the Tolpuddle Martyrs. They asked me if the fact that I had chosen to protest in *red* socks had any significance. I lied and said that I had chosen red because it was a symbol of revolution, then I blushed revolutionary red. I am turning into quite a liar recently.

Pandora's mother said I could call her Tania. Surely that is a Russian name? Her father said I could call him Ivan. He is very nice, he gave me a book to read; it is called *The Ragged Trousered Philanthropists*. I haven't looked through it yet but I'm quite interested in stamp collecting so I will read it tonight.

Washed red socks, put them on radiator to dry ready for the morning.

Monday   June 8th

Woke up, dressed, put red socks on before underpants or vest. Father stood at the door and wished me luck. Felt like a hero. Met Pandora and rest of committee at corner of our road; all of us were wearing red socks. Pandora's were lurex. She has certainly got guts! We sang "We shall not be moved" all the way to school. I felt a bit scared when we went through the gates but Pandora rallied us with shouts of encouragement.

Pop-eyed Scruton must have been tipped off because he was waiting in the fourth-year cloakroom. He was standing very still with his arms folded, staring with poached-egg eyes. He didn't speak, he just nodded us upstairs. All the red socks trooped upstairs. My heart was beating dead loud. He went silently into his office and sat at his desk and started tapping his teeth with a school pen. We just stood there.

He smiled in a horrible way then rang the bell on his desk. His secretary came in, he said, "Sit down and take a letter, Mrs. Claricoates." The letter was to our parents, it said:

Dear Mr. and Mrs. . . . . ,
It is my sad duty to inform you that your son/daughter has deliberately flaunted one of the rules of this school.
I take an extremely serious view of this contravention. I am therefore suspending your son/daughter for a period of one week. Young people today often lack sufficient moral guidance in the home, therefore I feel that it is my duty to take a firm stand in my school. If you wish to discuss the matter further with me do not hesitate to ring my secretary for an appointment.
Yours faithfully,
R. G. Scruton
Headmaster

Pandora started to say something about her O levels suffering but Scruton roared at her to shut up! Even Mrs. Claricoates jumped. Scruton said that we could wait until the letters had been typed, duplicated and signed and then we had better "hot foot it out of school." We waited outside Scruton's office. Pandora was crying (because she was angry and frustrated, she said). I put my arm round her a bit. Mrs. Claricoates gave us our letters. She smiled very kindly, it can't be very easy working for a despot.

We went round to Pandora's house but it was locked, so I said everyone could come round to my house. It was quite tidy for once, apart from the dog hairs. My father raged about the letter. He is supposed to be a Conservative but he is not being very conservative at the moment.

I can't help wishing that I had worn black socks on Friday.

Tuesday   June 9th
MOON'S FIRST QUARTER

My father saw Scruton today and told him that if he didn't allow me back to school in whatever color socks I liked he would protest to his MP. Mr. Scruton asked my father who his MP was. My father didn't know.

Wednesday   June 10th

Pandora and I are in love! It is official! She told Claire Neilson, who told Nigel, who told me.

I told Nigel to tell Claire to tell Pandora that I return her love. I am over the moon with joy and rapture. I can overlook the fact that Pandora smokes five Benson and Hedges a day and has her own lighter. When you are in love such things cease to matter.

Thursday   June 11th

Spent all day with my love. Can't write much, my hands are still trembling.

Friday   June 12th

Had a message from the school to say that Bert Baxter wanted to see me urgently. Went round with Pandora (we are inseparable). Bert is ill. He looked awful. Pandora made his bed up with clean sheets (she didn't seem to mind the smell) and I phoned the doctor. I described Bert's symptoms. Funny breathing, white face, sweating.

We tried to clean the bedroom up a bit, Bert kept

saying stupid things that didn't make sense. Pandora said that he was delirious. She held his hand until the doctor came. Dr. Patel was quite kind, he said that Bert needed oxygen. He gave me a number to ring for an ambulance, it seemed to take ages to come. I thought about how I had neglected Bert lately and I felt a real rat fink. The ambulancemen took Bert downstairs on a stretcher. They got stuck on the corner of the stairs and knocked a lot of empty beetroot jars over. Pandora and me cleared a path through the rubbish in the downstairs hall and they steered him through. He was wrapped in a big, fluffy red blanket before he went outside. Then they shut him up in the ambulance and he was sirened away. I had a big lump in my throat and my eyes were watering. It must have been caused by the dust.

Bert's house is very dusty.

Saturday   June 13th

Bert is in intensive care, he can't have visitors. I ring up every four hours to find out how he is. I pretend to be a relative. The nurses say things like "He is stable."

Sabre is staying with us. Our dog is staying at grandma's because it is scared of alsatians.

I hope Bert doesn't die. Apart from liking him, I have got nothing to wear to a funeral.

Still madly in love with P.

Sunday   June 14th
TRINITY SUNDAY

Went to see Bert, he has got tubes all over him. I took him a jar of beetroot for when he is better. The nurse put it in his locker. I took some "get well" cards, one from Pandora and me, one from my grandma, one from my father and one from Sabre.

Bert was asleep so I didn't stay long.

Monday June 15th

The Red Sock Committee has voted to give way to Scruton for the time being. We wear red socks underneath our black socks. This makes our shoes tight but we don't mind because a principle is involved.

Bert has made a slight improvement. He is awake more. I'll go round and see him tomorrow.

Tuesday June 16th

Bert has only got a few tubes left inside him now. He was awake when I went into his room. He didn't recognize me at first because I was wearing a mask and gown. He thought I was a doctor. He said, "Get these bleedin' tubes out of my private parts, I ain't an underground system." Then he saw it was me and asked how Sabre was. We had a long talk about Sabre's behavior problems, then the nurse came in and told me I had to go. Bert asked me to tell his daughters that he is on his death bed; he gave me half-a-crown for the phone calls! Two of them live in Australia! He said the numbers are written down in the back of his old army pay-book.

My father says that half-a-crown is roughly worth twelve and a half pence. I am keeping the half-a-crown. It has got a nice chunky feel about it and it will no doubt be a collector's item one day.

Wednesday June 17th
FULL MOON

Pandora and me searched Bert's house looking for his army pay-book. Pandora found a pile of brown and cream postcards that were very indecent. They were signed *"avec tout mon amour chéri, Lola."* I felt a bit funny after looking through them, so did Pandora. We exchanged our first really passionate kiss. I felt

like doing a French kiss but I don't know how it's
done so I had to settle for an ordinary English one.

No sign of the pay-book.

Thursday   June 18th

Bert is now tubeless. He is being moved into an ordinary ward tomorrow. I told him about not finding the
army pay-book, he said it doesn't matter now he
knows he's not dying.

Pandora came with me tonight. She got on well
with Bert; they talked about Blossom. Bert passed
on a few tips about grooming ponies. Then Pandora
went out to arrange the flowers she'd bought and
Bert asked me if I'd had my "leg over" yet. Sometimes
he is just a dirty old man who doesn't deserve visitors.

Friday   June 19th

Bert is on a big ward full of men with broken legs
and bandaged chests. He looks a lot better now
that he has got his teeth in. Some of the men whis-
tled at Pandora when she walked down the ward. I
wish she wasn't taller than me. Bert is in trouble
with the ward sister for getting beetroot juice on
the hospital sheets. He is supposed to be on a fluid
diet.

Saturday   June 20th

I hope Bert can come home soon. My father is fed up
with Sabre and my grandma is sick to death of our
dog.

Bert's consultant has told him to give up smoking
but Bert says at eighty-nine years old it is hardly
worth it. He has asked me to buy him twenty Woodbines and a box of matches. What shall I do?

Sunday   June 21st
FIRST AFTER TRINITY. FATHER'S DAY

Couldn't sleep last night for worrying about the
Woodbines. After much heart-searching decided not
to grant Bert's wish. Then went to the hospital to
find that Bert had bought his stinking fags from the
hospital trolley!

Just measured my thing. It has grown one centi-
metre. I might be needing it soon.

Monday June 22nd

Woke up with sore throat, couldn't swallow, tried to
shout downstairs but could only manage a croak.
Tried to attract my father's attention by banging on
my bedroom floor with school shoe but my father
shouted, "Stop that bloody banging." Eventually I
sent the dog downstairs with a message tucked inside its collar. I waited for ages, then I heard the dog
barking in the street. It hadn't delivered the message! I was close to despair. I had to get up to go to
the toilet but how I got there I don't know; it is all a
hazy blur. I stood at the top of the stairs and croaked
as loud as I could but my father had his Alma Cogan
records on so I was forced to go downstairs and tell
him I was ill. My father looked in my mouth and
said, "Christ Almighty, Adrian, your tonsils look like
Polaris missiles! What are you doing down here? Get
back into bed at once, you fool." He took my temperature: it was 112° Fahrenheit. By rights I should be
dead.

It is now five minutes to midnight, the doctor is
coming in the morning. I just pray that I can last out
until then. Should the worst happen, I hereby leave
all my worldly goods to Pandora Braithwaite of 69
Elm Tree Drive. I think I am of sound mind. It is very
hard to tell when you've got a temperature of 112°
Fahrenheit.

Tuesday   June 23rd

I have got tonsillitis. It is official. I am on antibiotics.
Pandora sits by my bed reading aloud to me. I wish
she wouldn't, every word is like a rock dropping on
my head.

Wednesday   June 24th

A "get well" card from my mother. Inside a five-pound
note. I asked my father to spend it on five bottles of
Lucozade.

Thursday   June 25th
MOON'S LAST QUARTER

I have delirious dreams about Lady Diana Spencer; I
hope I am better in time for the wedding. Temperature is still 112° Fahrenheit.
   My father can't cope with Sabre, so Pandora has
taken him home with her. (Sabre, not my father.)

Friday   June 26th

Doctor said our thermometer is faulty. I feel slightly
better.
   Got up for twenty minutes today. Watched *Play
School;* it was Carol Leader's turn, she is my favorite
presenter.
   Pandora brought me a "get well" card. She made it
herself with felt-tip pens. She signed it: "Forever
yours, Pan."
   I wanted to kiss her but my lips are still cracked.

Saturday   June 27th

Why hasn't my mother been to see me?

Sunday   June 28th
SECOND AFTER TRINITY

My mother has just left to catch the train for Sheffield. I am worn out with all the emotion. I am having a relapse.

Monday   June 29th

Pandora went to see Bert Baxter. She said the nurses
are getting fed up with him because he won't stay in
bed or do anything he is told to do. He is being dis-
charged on Thursday.

I long for the peace and quiet of a hospital ward. I
would be a perfect patient.

Pandora's father has put Sabre into kennels, it is
costing him three pounds a day, but Pandora's father
says that it is worth every penny.

Tuesday   June 30th

I am entering a period of convalescence. I will have
to take things very easily if I am to regain my former
vigor.

Wednesday   July 1st
DOMINION DAY, CANADA. NEW MOON

The truant officer came round this afternoon; he
caught me sitting in a deckchair in the front garden.
He didn't believe I was ill! He is reporting me to
the school! The fact that I was sipping Lucozade
whilst wearing pyjamas, dressing gown and slippers
seemed to have escaped him. I offered to show him
my yukky tonsils but he backed away and trod on
the dog's paw. The dog has got a low pain threshold
so it went a bit berserk. My father came out and sep-
arated them but things could get nasty for us.

Thursday   July 2nd

The doctor said I can go back to school tomorrow, de-
pending on how I feel. You can depend that I won't
feel up to it.

Friday   July 3rd

A brown-skinned family are moving into Mr. Lucas's
old house! I sat in my deckchair and had a good view
of their furniture being carried out of the removal
van. The brown-skinned ladies kept taking massive
cooking pots into the house so it looks as if they are a
large family. My father said that it was "the begin-
ning of the end of our street." Pandora is in the Anti-
Nazi League. She said she thinks that my father is a
possible racist.
    I am reading *Uncle Tom's Cabin*.

Saturday   July 4th
INDEPENDENCE DAY, USA

The street is full of brown-skinned people arriving or
departing in cars, vans and mini-buses. They keep
trooping in and out of Mr. Lucas's old house. My fa-

ther says they have probably got three families to each room.

Pandora and I are going round to welcome them to our district. We are determined to show that not all white people are racist fanatics.

Bert Baxter is still in hospital.

Sunday   July 5th
THIRD AFTER TRINITY

Stayed in bed until 6 P.M. There was no point in getting up. Pandora has gone to a gymkhana.

Monday   July 6th

Mrs. O'Leary is trying to organize a street party for the Royal Wedding. The only people to put their names down so far are the Singh family.

Tuesday   July 7th

Bert Baxter has escaped from hospital. He telephoned the National Council for Civil Liberties and they told him he could sign himself out, so he did. He is in our spare room. My father is going up the wall.

Pandora, Bert and I have put our names down for the street party. Bert is looking much better now that he can smoke as many Woodbines as he likes.

Pandora's father has been round to talk to my father about what to do about Bert and Sabre. They both got drunk and started arguing about politics. Bert banged on the floor and asked them to keep their voices down.

Wednesday   July 8th

My father is near to despair because of Bert's snoring. It doesn't bother me, I put Blu-tack in my ears.

Went to school today. I have decided to take Do-

mestic Science, Art, Woodwork and English O levels.
I am doing Geography, Math and History for CSE.

Pandora is taking nine O levels. But she has had
more advantages than me. She has been a member of
the library since she was three.

Thursday   July 9th

School breaks up for eight weeks tomorrow. Pandora
is going to Tunisia soon. How I will survive without
my love is anybody's guess. We have tried French
kissing but neither of us liked it, so we have gone
back to the English.

My skin is dead good. I think it must be a combina-
tion of being in love and Lucozade.

Friday   July 10th

It was magic at school today. All the teachers were in
good moods. A rumor went round that pop-eyed
Scruton was seen laughing but I didn't believe it myself.

Barry Kent climbed up the flagpole and flew a pair
of his mother's knickers in the breeze. Pandora said
it was probably the first airing they had had for
years.

Sean O'Leary is nineteen today. He has invited me
to his birthday party. It is only over the road so I
won't have far to go.

I am writing up my diary now just in case I have
one too many. People seem to get drunk just stepping
over the O'Leary's threshold.

Saturday   July 11th

First proper hangover. Aged fourteen years, five
months and nine days. Pandora put me to bed. She
gave me a fireman's lift up the stairs.

Sunday July 12th
FOURTH AFTER TRINITY

My father took me, Pandora and Bert to the Wagtails boarding kennels this morning. Mrs. Kane, the proprietor, has refused to keep Sabre any longer. It was very touching to see Bert and Sabre reunited. Mrs. Kane is a hard woman, she got very nasty when my father refused to pay Sabre's boarding fees, she kept smoothing her black mustache with her horny fingers and using unladylike language.

Bert said he won't be parted from Sabre again. He said that Sabre is his only friend in the world! After all *I* have done for him!! If it wasn't for me he would be a corpse by now, and Sabre would be an orphan living with the RSPCA.

Monday July 13th

Bert has been talking to Mrs. Singh! He speaks fluent Hindi! He says she has found some indecent magazines under the lino in the bathroom. An heirloom from that creep Lucas!

Mr. Singh is outraged. He has written to the estate agents to complain that his house has been defiled.

Bert showed me one of the magazines. They are not indecent in my opinion, but then I am a man of the world. I have put it under my mattress with the *Big and Bouncys*. It is called *Amateur Photographer*.

Tuesday July 14th

Bert's social worker came round tonight. She is called Katie Bell. She talked to Bert in a stupid way. She said that Bert had been offered a place in the Alderman Cooper Sunshine Home. Bert told her that he didn't want to go. Katie Bell said that he has got to go. Even my father said that he felt sorry for Bert.

But not sorry enough to invite Bert to live with us permanently I noticed!

Poor Bert, what will happen to him?

Wednesday   July 15th

Bert has moved in with the Singhs. Mr. Singh fetched Sabre's kennel so it is official. Bert looks dead happy. His favorite food is curry.

Pandora has allowed me to touch her bust. I promised not to tell anyone, but there was nothing to tell really. I couldn't tell where her bust began through all the layers of underclothes, dress, cardigan and anorak.

I am reading *Sex, The Facts,* by Dr. A. P. G. Haig.

Thursday   July 16th

11 A.M. My father got his redundancy check today. He did cowboy whoops up and down the hall. He has asked Doreen Slater to go out with him to celebrate. Guess who Maxwell's baby-sitter is going to be? Yes, dear diary, you guessed right! It is I!

11 P.M. Maxwell has only just gone to sleep, Pandora rang up at nine-thirty and asked how I was doing. I couldn't hear her properly because Maxwell was screaming so loudly. Pandora said I should try putting vodka in some hot milk and forcing it down his vile throat. I have just done it. And it worked.

He is not a bad kid when he is asleep.

Friday   July 17th
FULL MOON

My precious love leaves these shores tomorrow. I am going to the airport to see her off. I hope her plane won't suffer from metal fatigue. I have just checked the world map to see where Tunisia is, and I am most relieved to see that Pandora won't have to fly through the Bermuda triangle.

If anything happened to my love I would never smile again.

I have brought her a book to read during the flight. It is called *Crash!* by a bloke called William Goldenstein, III. It is very good on what to do if the worst happens.

Saturday July 18th

Pandora read the *Crash!* book in the coach on the way to the airport. When her flight was called she had slight hysterics and her father had to carry her up the steps. I waved to the plane until it had retreated into a large cloud, then I sadly got on a coach and came back home. How I will get through the next fortnight I don't know. Good-night, my Tunisian beauty.

Sunday July 19th
FIFTH AFTER TRINITY

Stayed in bed and looked at Tunisia on the map.

Monday July 20th

Not had a postcard from my love yet.

Tuesday July 21st

Bert came round this morning. He said that Tunisia is full of hazards.

Wednesday July 22nd

Why haven't I had a postcard yet? What can have happened?

Thursday July 23rd

Asked our postman about communications between Tunisia and England. He said that they were "diabolical"; he said that the Tunisian GPO depends on camels.

Friday   July 24th
MOON'S LAST QUARTER

Went to see Mr. Singh. He said that Tunisia is very unhygenic. Everybody but me seems to be familiar with Tunisia!

Saturday   July 25th

PANDORA! PANDORA! PANDORA!

> Oh! my love,
> My heart is yearning,
> My mouth is dry,
> My soul is burning.
> You're in Tunisia,
> I am here.
> Remember me and shed a tear.
> Come back tanned and brown and healthy.
> You're lucky that your dad is wealthy.

She will be back in six days.

Sunday   July 26th
SIXTH AFTER TRINITY

Went for tea at grandma's. I was sad and withdrawn because of Pandora's sojourn in Tunisia. Grandma asked if I was constipated. I nearly said something, but what's the use of trying to explain *love* to a woman of seventy-six who thinks the word is obscene?

Monday   July 27th

A camel postcard! It said:

Dearest,
Economic conditions here are quite dreadful. I was
going to buy you a present but instead I gave all
my money to a beggar.
You have such a generous heart, Adrian, that I feel
sure you will understand.
All my love into infinity.
　　For ever,
　　Pandora　　　　　　　　　　　　　　　　　X

Fancy giving my present money to a filthy, idle
beggar! Even our postman was disgusted.

Tuesday　July 28th

It's a wonder I have the strength to hold my pen! I have
been on the go all day with preparations for the Royal
Wedding street party. Mrs. O'Leary came over and
asked if I would help with the bunting. I said "I feel it
is my patriotic duty." Mrs. O'Leary said that if I
climbed the ladder she would pass the bunting up to
me. I was all right for the first four or five rungs but
then I made the mistake of looking down and I had a
vertigo attack, so Mrs. O'Leary did all the climbing. I
couldn't help noticing Mrs. O'Leary's knickers. They
are surprisingly sexy for someone who goes to church
every day and twice on Sundays. Black lace! With red-
satin ribbons! I got the feeling that Mrs. O'Leary knew
that I was looking at her knickers because she asked
me to call her Caitlin. I was glad when Mr. O'Leary
came to take over from me. Mr. and Mrs. Singh have
hung a huge Union Jack out of their front bedroom
window. Bert told me that it was one he stole when he
was in the army.

Our house is letting the street down. All my father
has done is pin a Charles and Diana tea towel to the
front door.

My father and I watched the Royal Wedding fire-
work display on television. All I can say is that I

tried to enjoy it but failed. My father said it was one
way of burning money. He is still bitter about being
out of work.

I hope the Prince remembers to remove the price
ticket off the bottom of his shoes; my father didn't at
his wedding. Everyone in the church read the ticket.
It said: "9½ reject, 10 shillings."

Wednesday   July 29th

ROYAL WEDDING DAY!!!!!

How proud I am to be English!

Foreigners must be as sick as pigs!

We truly lead the world when it comes to pag-
eantry! I must admit to having tears in my eyes
when I saw all the cockneys who had stood since
dawn, cheering heartily all the rich, well-dressed, famous people going by in carriages and Rolls-Royces.

Grandma and Bert Baxter came to our house to
watch the wedding because we have got a twenty-
four-inch color. They got on all right at first but
then Bert remembered he was a communist and
started saying anti-royalist things like "the idle rich"
and "parasites," so grandma sent him back to the
Singhs' color portable.

Prince Charles looked quite handsome in spite of his
ears. His brother is dead good-looking; it's a shame
they couldn't have swapped heads just for the day.
Lady Diana melted my heartstrings in her dirty white
dress. She even helped an old man up the aisle. I
thought it was very kind of her considering it was her
wedding day. Loads of dead famous people were there.
Nancy Reagan, Spike Milligan, Mark Phillips, etc., etc.
The Queen looked a bit jealous. I expect it was because
people weren't looking at *her* for a change.

The Prince had remembered to take the price ticket off his shoes. So that was one worry off my mind.

When the Prince and Di exchanged rings my

grandma started to cry. She hadn't brought her handkerchief so I went upstairs to get the spare toilet roll. When I came downstairs they were married. So I missed the Historic moment of their marriage!

I made a cup of tea during all the boring musical interval, but I was back in time to see that Kiwi woman singing. She has certainly got a good pair of lungs on her.

Grandma and I were just settling down to watch the happy couple's triumphant ride back to the palace when there was a loud banging on the front door. We ignored it so my father was forced to get out of bed and open the door. Bert and Mr. and Mrs. Singh and all the little Singhs came in asking for sanctuary. Their telly had broken down! My grandma tightened her lips, she is not keen on black, brown, yellow, Irish, Jewish or foreign people. My father let them all in, then took grandma home in the car. The Singhs and Bert gathered round the television talking in Hindi.

Mrs. Singh handed round some little cornish pasties. I ate one of them and had to drink a gallon of water. I thought my mouth had caught fire! They were not cornish pasties.

I watched television until the happy couple left Victoria station on a very strange-looking train. Bert said it was only strange-looking because it was clean.

Mrs. O'Leary came in and asked if she could borrow our old chairs for the street party. In my father's absence I agreed and helped to carry them out on to the pavement. Our street looked dead weird without cars and with flags and bunting flapping about.

Mrs. O'Leary and Mrs. Singh swept the street clean. Then we all helped to put the tables and chairs out into the middle of the road. The women did all the work, the men stood around on the pavement drinking too much and making jokes about Royal Nuptials.

Mr. Singh put his stereo speakers out of his lounge

windows and we listened to a Des O'Connor LP whilst we set the tables with sandwiches, jam tarts, sausage rolls and sausages on sticks. Then everyone in our street was given a funny hat by Mrs. O'Leary and we sat down to eat. At the end of the tea Mr. Singh made a speech about how great it was to be British. Everyone cheered and sang "Land of Hope and Glory." But only Mr. Singh knew all the words. Then my father came back with four party packs of light ale and two dozen paper cups, and soon everyone was acting in an undignified manner.

Mr. O'Leary tried to teach Mrs. Singh an Irish jig but he kept getting tangled up in her sari. I put my Abba LP on and turned the volume up high and soon even the old people of forty and over were dancing! When the street lamps came on Sean O'Leary climbed up and put red, white and blue crepe paper over the bulbs to help the atmosphere and I fetched our remaining candles and put them on the tables. Our street looked quite Bohemian.

Bert told some lies about the war, my father told jokes. The party went on until one o'clock in the morning!

Normally they get a petition up if you clear your throat after eleven o'clock at night!

I didn't dance, I was an amused, cynical observer. Besides my feet were aching.

Thursday   July 30th

I have seen the Royal Wedding repeats seven times on television.

Friday   July 31st
NEW MOON

Sick to death of Royal Wedding.

Pandora, the beggar's friend, is coming home tomorrow.

Saturday　August 1st

Postcard from my mother, she wants me to go on holiday with her and creep Lucas. They are going to Scotland. I hope they enjoy themselves.

Pandora's flight has been delayed because of a baggage-handlers' strike in Tunis.

Sunday　August 2nd
SEVENTH AFTER TRINITY

The baggage-handlers are still on strike and Pandora's father has had his American Express card stolen by a beggar!

Pandora said that her mother has been bitten by a camel but is recovering in the Ladies' toilet at Tunis airport. It was wonderful to hear Pandora's voice on the telephone, we talked to each other for over half an hour. How clever it was of her to arrange a reverse-charge call from Tunisia!

Monday　August 3rd
BANK HOLIDAY IN SCOTLAND AND REP. OF IRELAND

The Tunisian baggage-handlers have agreed to go to arbitration. Pandora says that with luck she'll be home by Thursday.

Tuesday　August 4th

The Tunisian baggage-handlers can see light at the end of the tunnel.

Pandora is surviving on packets of dates and Polo mints.

Wednesday　August 5th

The Tunisian baggage-handlers are now handling baggage. *Pandora home FRIDAY EVENING!*

Thursday   August 6th

My father refused a reverse-charge call from Tunisia. Our lines of communication have been cut.

Friday   August 7th
MOON'S FIRST QUARTER

I rang Tunisia whilst my father was in the bath. He shouted down to ask whom I was phoning. I told a lie. I said I was phoning the speaking clock.

Pandora's flight left safely. She should be home around midnight.

Saturday   August 8th

At 7 A.M. Pandora rang from from St. Pancras station. She said that due to electrification of the track at Flitwick she would be delayed.

I got dressed and went down to the station, got a platform ticket, waited on platform two for six cold, lonely hours. Went home to find a note from Pandora. This is what is said:

Adrian,
I confess to feeling heartbroken at your apparent coldness concerning my arrival. I felt sure that we would have an emotional reunion on platform three. But it was not to be.
   Adieu,
   Pandora

Went to Pandora's house. Explained. Had an emotional reunion behind her father's tool shed.

Sunday   August 9th
EIGHTH AFTER TRINITY

Touched Pandora's bust again. This time I think I felt something soft. My thing keeps growing and shrinking, it seems to have a life of its own. I can't control it.

Monday   August 10th

Pandora and I went to the swimming baths this morning. Pandora looked superb in her white string bikini. She has gone the same color as Mrs. Singh. I didn't trust my thing to behave so I sat in the spectators' gallery and watched Pandora diving off the highest diving board. Got back to my house. Showed her my black room. Lit a joss stick. Put Abba LP on, sneaked a bottle of Sanatogen upstairs. We indulged in a bit of light petting but then Pandora developed a headache and went home to rest.

I was racked with sexuality but it wore off when I helped my father put manure on our rose bed.

Tuesday   August 11th

Got another postcard from my mother.

Dear Aidy,
You've no idea how much I long to see you. The mothering bond is as strong as ever. I know you feel threatened by my involvement with Bimbo, but really, Aidy, there is no need. Bimbo fulfills my sexual needs. No more, no less. So, Aidy, grow up and come to Scotland.
Lots of love,
Pauline (mother)

P.S. We leave on the fifteenth. Catch 8:22 train to Sheffield.

The postman said that if my mother was his wife he would give her a good thrashing. He doesn't know my mother. If anybody laid a finger on *her* she would beat them to pulp.

Wednesday August 12th

Pandora thinks a trial separation will do us good. She says our light to medium petting will turn quite heavy soon. I must admit that the strain is having a detrimental affect on my health. I have got no energy and my sleep is constantly interrupted with dreams about Pandora's white bikini and Mrs. O'Leary's knickers.

I might go to Scotland after all.

Thursday August 13th

My father has decided to go to Skegness on the fifteenth. He has booked a four-berth caravan. He is taking Doreen and Maxwell with him! He expects me to go!

If I go people will automatically assume that Doreen is my mother and Maxwell is my brother!

I am going to Scotland.

Friday August 14th

Had tragic last night with Pandora. We have both sworn to be true. I have done all my packing. The dog has been taken round to grandma's with fourteen tins of Pedigree Chum and a giant sack of Winalot.

I am taking *Escape from Childhood*, by John Holt, to read on the train.

Saturday August 15th
FULL MOON

My father, Stick Insect and Maxwell House saw me off at the station. My father didn't mind a bit that I chose to go to Scotland instead of Skegness. In fact he looked dead cheerful. The train journey was terrible. I had to stand all the way to Sheffield. I spoke to a lady in a wheelchair who was in the guard's van. She was very nice, she said that the only good thing about being handicapped was that you always got a seat in trains. Even if it *was* in the guard's van.

My mother and creep Lucas met me at Sheffield. My mother looked dead thin and has started dressing in clothes that are too young for her. Lucas creep was wearing jeans! His belly was hanging over his belt. I pretended to be asleep until we got to Scotland.

Lucas mauled my mother about even whilst he was driving.

We are at a place called Loch Lubnaig. I am in bed in a log cabin. My mother and Lucas have gone to the village to try to buy cigarettes. At least that is their story.

Sunday August 16th
NINTH AFTER TRINITY

There is a loch in front of the cabin and a pine forest and a mountain behind the cabin. There is nothing to do. It is dead boring.

Monday August 17th

Did some washing in a log cabin launderette. Spoke to an American tourist called Hamish Mancini; he is the same age as me. His mother is on her honeymoon for the fourth time.

Tuesday August 18th

Rained all day.

Wednesday August 19th

Sent postcards. Phoned Pandora, reversed charges. Her father refused to accept them.

Thursday August 20th

Played cards with Hamish Mancini. His mother and stepfather and my mother and her lover have gone to see a waterfall in the car. Big deal!

Friday   August 21st

Walked two and a half miles into Callander to buy
Mars bar. Played on Space Invaders. Came back, had
tea. Phoned Pandora from log cabin phone box. Reversed charges. She still loves me. I still love her.
Went to bed.

Saturday   August 22nd
MOON'S LAST QUARTER

Went to see Rob Roy's grave. Saw it, came back.

Sunday   August 23rd
TENTH AFTER TRINITY

My mother has made friends with a couple called Mr.
and Mrs. Ball. They have gone off to Stirling Castle.
Mrs. Ball has got a daughter who is a writer. I asked
her how her daughter qualified to be one. Mrs. Ball
said that her daughter was dropped on her head as a
child and has been "a bit queer" ever since.

It is Mrs. Ball's birthday so they all came back to
our log cabin to celebrate. I complained about the
noise at 1 A.M., 2 A.M., 3 A.M. and 4 A.M. At 5 A.M. they
decided to climb the mountain! I pointed out to them
that they were blind drunk, too old, unqualified, un-
fit and lacking in any survival techniques, had no
first-aid kit, weren't wearing stout boots, and had no
compass, map or sustaining hot drinks.

My protests fell on deaf ears. They all climbed the
mountain, came down and were cooking eggs and
bacon by 11:30 A.M.

As I write, Mr. and Mrs. Ball are canoeing on the
loch. They must be on drugs.

Monday   August 24th

Went to Edinburgh. Saw the castle, the toy museum,
the art gallery. Bought a haggis. Came back to log

cabin, read *Glencoe,* by John Prebble. We are going there tomorrow.

Tuesday   August 25th

The massacre of Glencoe took place on February 13, 1692. On February 14, John Hill wrote to the Earl of Tweeddale, "I have ruined Glencoe."

He was dead right, there is nothing there. Glasgow tomorrow.

Wednesday   August 26th

We drove through Glasgow at 11 A.M. in the morning yet I counted twenty-seven drunks in one mile! All the shops except the DIY shops had grilles at the windows. Off-licenses had rolls of barbed wire and broken glass on their roofs. We had a walk round for a bit, then my mother nagged Lucas creep into taking her to the Glasgow art gallery. I intended to sit in the car and read *Glencoe,* but because of all the drunks staggering around I reluctantly followed them inside.

How glad I am that I did! I might have gone through life without having an important cultural experience!

Today I saw Salvador Dali's painting of the Crucifixion!!! *The real one!* Not a reproduction!

They have hung it at the end of a corridor so that it changes as you get nearer to it. When you are finally standing up close to it you feel like a midget. It is absolutely fantastic!

Huge! With dead good colors and Jesus looks like a real bloke. I bought six postcards of it from the museum but of course it is not the same as the real thing.

One day I will take Pandora to see it. Perhaps on our honeymoon.

Thursday August 27th

Oban today. Bumped into Mr. and Mrs. Swallow who
live in the next street to me. Everyone kept saying,
"It's a small world, isn't it?" Mrs. Swallow asked creep
Lucas how his wife was. Lucas told her that his wife
had left him for another woman. Then everyone
blushed and said "what a small world it was" and
parted company. My mother went mad at Lucas. She
said "Do you have to tell everyone?" and "How do you
think I feel living with a lesbian's estranged husband?" Lucas whined on for a bit but then my mother started looking like my grandma. So he kept quiet.

Friday August 28th

Fort William today. Ben Nevis was another disap-
pointment. I couldn't tell where it began or stopped.
The other mountains and hills clutter it up. Lucas
fell in the burn (Scottish for "little river") but unfortu-
nately it was too shallow to drown in.

Saturday August 29th
FULL MOON

Went for a walk around the loch with Hamish
Mancini. He told me that he thinks his mother is
heading for her fifth divorce. He is going home tonight; he has got an appointment with his analyst in
New York on Monday morning.

I have finished my packing and I am waiting for
my mother and creep Lucas to come back from their
furtive love-making somewhere in the pine forest.

We leave at dawn.

Sunday August 30th
ELEVENTH AFTER TRINITY

I made Lucas stop for souvenirs at Gretna Green. I
bought Pandora a pebble shaped like an otter, Bert a
tam-o'-shanter, the dog a tartan bow for its neck,

grandma a box of tartan fudge, Stick Insect tartan biscuits, Maxwell a tartan sweet dummy. I bought my father a tartan tea towel.

I bought myself a tartan scribbling pad. I am determined to become a writer.

Here is an extract from "My thoughts on Scotland" written on the M6 at 120 mph:

The hallowed mist rolls away leaving Scotland's majestic peaks revealed in all their majesty. A shape in the translucent sky reveals itself to be an eagle, that majestic bird of prey. Talons clawing, it lands on a loch, rippling the quiet majesty of the turbulent waters. The eagle pauses only to dip its majestic beak into the aqua before spreading its majestic wings and flying away to its magisterial nest high in the barren, arid, grassless hills.

The Highland cattle. Majestic horned beast of the glens lowers its brown-eyed shaggy-haired majestic head as it ruminates on the mysteries of Glencoe.

There are a couple too many "majestics." But I think it reads rather well. I will send it to the BBC when it's finished. Got home at 6 P.M. Too tired to write more.

Monday   August 31st
BANK HOLIDAY IN UK (EXCEPT SCOTLAND)

Everyone is broke. The banks are closed and my father can't remember the secret code on his plastic moneycard. He had the nerve to borrow five pounds from Bert Baxter. Fancy asking an old age pensioner for money! It lacks dignity.

Pandora and I are now insanely in love! The separation only served to fuel our passion. Our hormones are stirred every time we meet. Pandora slept with the otter pebble in her hand last night. How I wish the otter pebble could have been me.

Tuesday   September 1st

Mr. Singh has had to return to India to look after his aged parents, so Bert has been told that he will have to move back into his dirty old house! Mr. Singh says that he cannot trust his womenfolk to be alone in the house with Bert. How stupid can you get? Bert doesn't mind too much; he said that it is "quite a compliment."

Pandora and I are going to clean Bert's house and help him move back. He owes the council two hundred and ninety-four pounds in rent arrears. He has got to pay the arrears off at fifty pence a week, so it is a certainty that Bert will die in debt.

Wednesday   September 2nd

Pandora and I went to look at Bert's house today. It is a truly awesome sight. If Bert took all his empty beer bottles back to the off-license he might get enough money on the empties to pay off his rent arrears.

Thursday   September 3rd

My father helped us to move all of the furniture out of the ground floor of Bert's house, the woodworms came out to sunbathe. When we lifted the carpets we discovered that Bert had been walking about on a layer of dirt, old newspapers, hairpins, marbles and decomposed mice for years. We hung the carpets on the washing line and beat them all afternoon, but the dust billowed out non-stop. Pandora got excited at about 5 P.M., she claimed she could see a pattern emerging on one carpet, but closer examination showed it to be squashed fairy cake. We are going back tomorrow with Pandora's mother's carpet-shampooer. Pandora said it has been tested by *Which?* but I bet it has never had to clean a filthy hovel like Bert Baxter's before.

Friday September 4th

I have just witnessed a miracle! This morning Bert's carpets were dark gray in color. Now one is a red Axminster and the other is a blue Wilton. The carpets are hanging on the clothes line to dry. We have scraped all the floors clean and washed the furniture down with a fungicide disinfectant. Pandora took the curtains down but they fell to pieces before she could get them to the sink. Bert has been sitting in a deckchair criticizing and complaining. He can't see what's wrong with living in a dirty house.

What *is* wrong with living in a dirty house?

Saturday September 5th

My father took Bert's bottles to the off-license this morning. The boot, back seat and floor of the car were filled with them. The car stank of brown ale. He ran out of petrol on the way and called the AA. The AA man was most uncivil, he said it wasn't the Automobile Association my father needed, it was Alcoholics Anonymous!

Sunday September 6th
TWELFTH AFTER TRINITY. MOON'S FIRST QUARTER

Bert's house looks great. Everything is dead clean and shiny. We have moved his bed into the lounge so that he can watch television in bed. Pandora's mother has done very artistic arrangements with flowers, and Pandora's father has made an alsatian flap in the back door so that Bert doesn't keep having to get up to answer the door to Sabre.

Bert is moving back in tomorrow.

Monday September 7th
LABOR DAY, USA AND CANADA

An airmail letter from Hamish Mancini.

Hi Aid!

Howya doin'? I hope the situation Pandora-wise is
ongoing! She sounds kinda zappy! Scotland blew
my mind! It was so far out as to be nuked! You're a
great human being, Aid. I guess I was kinda trau-
matized when we rapped but Dr. Eagelburger (my
shrink) is doing great things with my libido.
Mom's really wiped out right now, turns out number five is a TV and has a better collection of
Calvin Kleins than she do! Don't you think the fall
is a drag? Son-of-a-bitch leaves everywhere!

  See you, Buddy!!!
  Hamish

I showed it to Pandora, my father and Bert but nobody understands it. Bert doesn't like Americans because it took them too long to come into the war or
something.

Bert now in his clean house. He hasn't said thank-
you, but he seems happy.

Tuesday   September 8th

Lousy stinking school on Thursday. I tried my old
uniform on but I have outgrown it so badly that my
father is being forced to buy me a new one tomorrow.

He is going up the wall but I can't help it if my
body is in a growth period, can I? I am only five centimeters shorter than Pandora now. My thing remains
static at twelve centimeters.

Wednesday   September 9th

Grandma phoned, she has found out about Doreen
and Maxwell going to Skegness. She is never speaking to my father again.

Here is my shopping list:

Blazer   £29.99

2 pairs gray trousers	£23.98
2 white shirts	£11.98
2 gray pullovers	£7.98
3 pairs black socks	£2.37
1 pair PE shorts	£4.99
1 PE vest	£3.99
1 track suit	£11.99
1 pair training shoes	£7.99
1 pair football boots and studs	£11.99
1 pair football socks	£2.99
Football shorts	£4.99
Football shirt	£7.99
Adidas sports bag	£4.99
1 pair black shoes	£15.99
1 calculator	£6.99
Pen and pencil set	£3.99
Geometry set	£2.99

My father can easily spare a hundred pounds. His redundancy payment must have been huge, so why he is lying on his bed moaning I don't know. He is just a mean skinflint! He hasn't paid with *real* money anyway! He used his American Express card.

Pandora admired me in my new uniform. She says she thinks I stand a good chance of being made a prefect.

Thursday   September 10th

A proud start to the new term. I am a prefect! My first duty is as late duty prefect. I have to wait by the gap in the railings and take the name of anyone sneaking late into school. Pandora is also a prefect. She is in charge of silence in the dinner queue.

My new timetable was given to me today by my new form tutor, Mr. Dock. It includes my O level and CSE lessons, and it is compulsory to do Math, English, PE and Comparative Religion. But they do

give you a choice of Cultural and Creative subjects.
So I have chosen Media Studies (dead easy, just reading newspapers and watching telly) and Parentcraft
(just learning about sex, I hope). Mr. Dock also
teaches English Literature, so we are bound to get
on, by now I am surely the best-read kid in the
school. I will be able to help him out if he gets stuck.

Asked my father for five pounds fifty for school
trip to the British Museum. He went berserk and
said, "What happened to free education?" I told him
that I didn't know.

Friday September 11th

Had a long talk with Mr. Dock. I explained that I was
a one-parent-family child with an unemployed, bad-
tempered father. Mr. Dock said he wouldn't care if I
was the offspring of a black, lesbian, one-legged
mother and an Arab, leprous, humpbacked-dwarf father so long as my essays were lucid, intelligent and
unpretentious. So much for pastoral care!

Saturday September 12th

Wrote lucid, intelligent and unpretentious essay
about Scottish wild life in the morning. In afternoon
did shopping in Sainsbury's with my father. Saw
Rick Lemon dithering at the fruit counter; he said se-
lecting fruit was an "overtly political act." He re-
jected South African apples, French golden delicious
apples, Israeli oranges, Tunisian dates, and American grapefruits. In the end he selected English rhubarb, "Although," he said, "the shape was phallic,
possibly sexist." His girlfriend, Tit (short for Titia),
was cramming the trolley with pulses and rice. She
had a long skirt on but now and again I caught a
glimpse of her hairy ankles. My father said he pre-
ferred a nice shaven leg any day. My father likes

stockings, suspenders, mini-skirts and low neck-
lines! He is dead old-fashioned.

Sunday   September 13th
THIRTEENTH AFTER TRINITY

Went to see Blossom. Pandora doesn't ride her now
because her feet drag on the ground. Pandora is having a proper horse delivered next week. It is called
Ian Smith. The people who are selling it used to live
in Africa, in Zimbabwe.

*Tomorrow is my mother's birthday. She is thirty-
seven.*

Monday   September 14th
FULL MOON

Phoned my mother before school. There was no answer. I expect she was lying in bed with that stinking rat Lucas.

School dinners are complete crap now. Gravy
seems to have been phased out along with custard
and hot puddings. A typical menu is: hamburger,
baked beans, chips, carton of yoghurt or a doughnut.
It's not enough to build healthy bone and sinew. I am
considering making a protest to Mrs. Thatcher. It
won't be our fault if we grow up apathetic and
lacking in moral fibre. Perhaps Mrs. Thatcher wants
us to be too weak to demonstrate in years to come.

Tuesday   September 15th

Barry Kent has been late three times in one week. So it
is my unfortunate duty to report him to Mr. Scruton.

Unpunctuality is the sign of a disordered brain. So
he cannot go unpunished.

Wednesday   September 16th

Our form is going to the British Museum on Friday. Pandora and I are going to sit together on the coach. She is bringing her *Guardian* from home so that we can have some privacy.

Thursday   September 17th

Had a lecture on the British Museum from Ms. Fossington-Gore. She said it was a "fascinating treasure house of personkind's achievements." Nobody listened to the lecture. Everyone was watching the way she felt her left breast whenever she got excited.

Friday   September 18th

2 A.M. Just got back from London. Coach driver suffered from motorway madness on the motorway. I am too shaken by the experience to be able to give a lucid or intelligent account of the day.

Saturday   September 19th

The school may well want a clear account by an unprejudiced observer of what happened on the way to, during, and coming back from our trip to London. I am the only person qualified. Pandora, for all her qualities, does not possess my nerves of steel.

Class Four-D's Trip to the British Museum
7 A.M. Boarded coach.
7:05 Ate packed lunch, drank low-calorie drink.
7:10 Coach stopped for Barry Kent to be sick.
7:20 Coach stopped for Claire Neilson to go to the Ladies.
7:30 Coach left school drive.
7:35 Coach returned to school for Ms. Fossington-Gore's handbag.
7:40 Coach driver observed to be behaving oddly.

7:45 Coach stopped for Barry Kent to be sick again.

7:55 Approached motorway.

8 A.M. Coach driver stopped coach and asked everyone to stop giving *V* signs to lorry drivers.

8:10 Coach driver loses temper, refuses to drive on motorway until "bloody teachers control kids."

8:20 Ms. Fossington-Gore gets everyone sitting down.

8:25 Drive on to motorway.

8:30 Everyone singing "Ten Green Bottles."

8:35 Everyone singing "Ten Green Snotrags."

8:45 Coach driver stops singing by shouting very loudly.

9:15 Coach driver pulls in at service station and is observed to drink heavily from hip-flask.

9:30 Barry Kent hands round bars of chocolate stolen from self-service shop at service station. Ms. Fossington-Gore chooses Bounty bar.

9:40 Barry Kent sick in coach.

9:50 Two girls sitting near Barry Kent are sick.

9:51 Coach driver refuses to stop on motorway.

9:55 Ms. Fossington-Gore covers sick in sand.

9:56 Ms. Fossington-Gore sick as a dog.

10:30 Coach crawls along on hard shoulder, all other lanes closed for repairs.

11:30 Fight breaks out on back seat as coach approaches end of motorway.

11:45 Fight ends. Ms. Fossington-Gore finds first-aid kit and sees to wounds. Barry Kent is punished by sitting next to driver.

11:50 Coach breaks down at Swiss Cottage.

11:55 Coach driver breaks down in front of AA man.

12:30 Class Four-D catch London bus to St. Pancras.

1 P.M. Class Four-D walk from St. Pancras through Bloomsbury.

1:15 Ms. Fossington-Gore knocks on door of Tavistock House, asks if Dr. Laing will give Barry Kent a quick going-over. Dr. Laing in America on lecture tour.

1:30 Enter British Museum. Adrian Mole and Pandora Braithwaite awestruck by evidence of heritage of World Culture. Rest of class Four-D run berserk, laughing at nude statues and dodging curators.

2:15 Ms. Fossington-Gore in state of collapse. Adrian Mole makes reverse-charge phone call to headmaster. Headmaster in dinner-lady strike-meeting, can't be disturbed.

3 P.M. Curators round up class Four-D and make them sit on steps of museum.

3:05 American tourists photograph Adrian Mole saying he is a "cute English schoolboy."

3:15 Ms. Fossington-Gore recovers and leads class Four-D on sightseeing tour of London.

4 P.M. Barry Kent jumps in fountain at Trafalgar Square, as predicted by Adrian Mole.

4:30 Barry Kent disappears, last seen heading towards Soho.

4:35 Police arrive, take Four-D to mobile police unit, arrange coach back. Phone parents about new arrival time. Phone headmaster at home. Claire Neilson has hysterical fit. Pandora Braithwaite tells Ms. Fossington-Gore she is a disgrace to teaching profession. Ms. Fossington-Gore agrees to resign.

6 P.M. Barry Kent found in sex shop. Charged with theft of "grow-it-big" cream and two "ticklers."

7 P.M. Coach leaves police station with police escort.

7:30 Police escort waves goodbye.

7:35 Coach driver begs Pandora Braithwaite to keep order.

7:36 Pandora Braithwaite keeps order.

8 P.M. Ms. Fossington-Gore drafts resignation.

8:30 Coach driver afflicted by motorway madness.

8:40 Arrive back. Tyres burning. Class Four-D

struck dumb with terror. Ms. Fossington-Gore led off by Mr. Scruton. Parents up in arms. Coach driver charged by police.

Sunday   September 20th
FOURTEENTH AFTER TRINITY. MOON'S LAST QUARTER

Keep having anxiety attacks every time I think about London, culture or the M1. Pandora's parents are lodging an official complaint to everyone they can think of.

Monday   Setpember 21st

Mr. Scruton complimented Pandora and I on our leadership qualities. Ms. Fossington-Gore is on sick leave. All future school trips have been canceled.

Tuesday   September 22nd

The police have dropped charges against coach driver because there is "evidence of severe provocation." The sex shop are not pressing charges either because officially Barry Kent is a child. A child! Barry Kent has never been a child.

Wednesday   September 23rd

Mr. Scruton has now read my report on the trip to London. He gave me two merit marks for it!

It was on the news today that the British Museum is thinking of banning school parties.

Thursday   September 24th

Pandora and I are enjoying the last of the autumn together by walking through leaves and sniffing bonfires. This is the first year I have been able to pass a horse-chestnut tree without throwing a stick at it.

Pandora says I am maturing very quickly.

Friday September 25th

Went out conkering with Nigel tonight. I found five big beauties and smashed Nigel's into pulp. Ha! Ha! Ha!

Saturday September 26th

Took Blossom to see Bert. He can't walk far these days.

Blossom is being sold to a rich family, a girl called Camilla is going to learn to ride on her. Pandora says Camilla is so posh as to be unintelligible. Bert was dead sad, he said, "You and me will both end up in the knacker's yard, gel."

Sunday September 27th
FIFTEENTH AFTER TRINITY

Blossom went off at 10:30 A.M. I gave her a sixteen-pence apple to take her mind off the heartbreak. Pandora ran after the little horse-box shouting, "I've changed my mind," but it carried on.

Pandora has also changed her mind about Ian Smith. She never wants to see another pony or horse again. She is guilt-ridden about selling Blossom.

Ian Smith turned up at 2:30 P.M. and was turned away. There was an evil look on his black face as he stood in his horse-box and was driven away. Pandora's father is going to his bank early tomorrow to cancel the check he wrote out last Thursday. There was an evil look on his face as well.

Monday   September 28th
NEW MOON

Bert has got something wrong with his legs. The doctor says he needs daily nursing. I went in today but he is too heavy for me to lug about. The district nurse thinks that Bert will be better off in the Alderman Cooper Sunshine Home. But I don't think he will. I pass by it on my way to school. It looks like a museum. The old people look like the exhibits.

Bert, you are dead old.
Fond of Sabre, beetroot and Woodbines.
We have nothing in common,
I am fourteen and a half,
You are eighty-nine.
You smell, I don't.
Why we are friends
Is a mystery to me.

Tuesday   September 29th

Bert doesn't get on with his district nurse. He says he doesn't like having his privates mauled about by a woman. Personally, I wouldn't mind it.

Wednesday   September 30th

I am glad September is nearly over, it has been nothing but trouble. Blossom gone. Pandora sad. Bert on his last legs. My father still out of work. My mother still besotted with creep Lucas.

Thursday   October 1st
7:30 A.M. Just woke up to find chin covered in spots!
How can I face Pandora?
10 P.M. Avoided Pandora all day but she caught up
with me in school dinners. I tried to eat with my
hand over my chin but it proved very difficult. I confessed to her during the yoghurt. She accepted my
disability very calmly. She said it made no difference
to our love but I couldn't help thinking that her
kisses lacked their usual passion as we were saying
good-night after youth club.

Friday   October 2nd

6 P.M. I am very unhappy and have once again
turned to great literature for solace. It's no surprise
to me that intellectuals commit suicide, go mad or
die from drink. We feel things more than other people. We know the world is rotten and that chins are
ruined by spots. I am reading *Progress, Coexistence
and Intellectual Freedom*, by Andrei D. Sakharov.

It is "an inestimably important document" according to the cover.
11:30 P.M. Progress, Coexistence and Intellectual
Freedom is inestimably *boring*, according to me,
Adrian Mole.

I disagree with Sakharov's analysis of the causes
of the revivalism of Stalinism. We are doing Russia
at school so I speak from knowledge.

Saturday   October 3rd

Pandora is cooling off. She didn't turn up at Bert's today. I had to do his cleaning on my own.

Went to Sainsbury's as usual in the afternoon;
they are selling Christmas cakes. I feel that my life
is slipping away.

I am reading *Wuthering Heights*. It is brilliant. If I

could get Pandora up somewhere high, I'm sure we could regain our old passion.

Sunday   October 4th
SIXTEENTH AFTER TRINITY

Persuaded Pandora to put her name down for the youth club's mountain survival course in Derbyshire. Rick Lemon is sending an equipment list and permission form to our parents. Or in my case to my parent. I have only got two weeks to reach peak condition. I try to do fifty press-ups a night. I try to do them but fail. Seventeen is my best so far.

Monday   October 5th

Bert has been kidnapped by Social Services! They are keeping him at the Alderman Cooper Sunshine Home. I have been to see him. He shares a room with an old man called Thomas Bell. They have both got their names on their ashtrays. Sabre has got a place in the RSPCA hostel.

Our dog has gone missing. It is a portent of doom.

Tuesday   October 6th
MOON'S FIRST QUARTER

Pandora and I went to visit Bert, but it was a waste of time really.

His room had a strange effect on us, it made us not want to talk about anything. Bert says he is going to sue Social Services, for depriving him of his rights. He says he has to go to bed at nine-thirty! It is not fair because he is used to staying up until after *The Epilogue*. We passed the lounge on our way out. The old people sat around the walls in high chairs. The television was on but nobody was watching it, the old people looked as though they were thinking.

Social Services have painted the walls orange to

try to cheer the old people up. It doesn't seem to have
worked.

Wednesday   October 7th

Thomas Bell died in the night. Bert says that nobody
leaves the home alive. Bert is the oldest inmate. He
is dead worried about dying. He is now the only man
in the entire home. Pandora says that women outlive
men. She says it is a sort of bonus because women
have to suffer more earlier on.
 Our dog is still missing. I have put an advert in Mr.
Cherry's shop.

Thursday   October 8th

Bert is still alive so I took Sabre to visit him today.
We propped Bert up at the window of his room and
we waved to Sabre who was on the lawn outside.
Dogs are not allowed inside the home. It is another of
their poxy rules.
 Our dog is still missing, now presumed dead.

Friday   October 9th

The matron of the home says that if Bert is dead good
he can come out for the day on Sunday. He is coming
to our house for Sunday dinner and tea. The phone
bill has come. I have hidden it under my mattress. It
is for £289.19p.

Saturday   October 10th

I am really worried about our dog. It has vanished off
the face of our suburb. Nigel, Pandora and I have
walked the cul-de-sacs looking for it.
 Another worry is my father. He lies in bed until
noon, then fries a mess in a pan, eats it, opens a can
or bottle, then sits and watches *After Noon Plus*. He
is making no attempt to find another job. He needs a

bath, a haircut and a shave. It is Parents' Night at
school next Tuesday. I have taken his best suit to the
cleaner's.

I bought a book from W. H. Smith's, it was only
five pence. It was written by an unsuccessful writer
called Drake Fairclough; it is called *Cordon Bleu for
the Elderly*. Bert is coming tomorrow. Pandora's father has ordered their phone to be taken out. He has
found out about the reverse-charge calls.

Sunday　October 11th
SEVENTEENTH AFTER TRINITY

BERT'S VISIT

I got up early this morning and cleared the furniture out of the hall so that Bert's wheelchair had
room to maneuver. I made my father a cup of coffee
and took it up to him in bed, then I started cooking
geriatric *coq au vin*. I left it on to boil whilst I went
back upstairs to reawaken my father. When I got
downstairs I knew that I'd made a mess of the *coq au
vin*. All the vinegar had boiled away and left burnt
chicken. I was most disappointed because I was
thinking of making my debut as a cook today. I
wanted to impress Pandora with my multi talents, I
think she is getting a bit bored with my conversation
about great literature and the Norwegian leather industry.

Bert insisted on bringing a big trunk with him
when Pandora's father picked him up at the home.
So what with that and his wheelchair and Bert
sprawling all over the back seat I was forced to
crouch in the hatch of the hatchback car. It took ages
to get Bert out of the car and into his wheelchair. Almost as long as it took me to get my father out of bed.

Pandora's father stayed for a quick drink, then a
pre-lunch one, then a chaser, then one for the road.
Then he had one to prove that he never got drunk

during the day. Pandora's lips started to go thin (women must teach young girls to do this). Then she confiscated her father's car keys and phoned her mother to come and collect the car. I had to endure watching my father do his imitation of some bloke called Frank Sinatra singing "One for my baby and one more for the road." Pandora's father pretended to be the bartender with our Tupperware custard jug. They were both drunkenly singing when Pandora's mother came in. Her lips were so thin they had practically disappeared. She ordered Pandora and Pandora's father out into the car, then she said that it was about time my father pulled himself together. She said she knew my father felt humiliated, alienated and bitter because he was unemployed, but that he was setting a bad example to an impressionable adolescent. Then she drove off at 10 mph. Pandora blew me a kiss through the rear windscreen.

I object strongly! Nothing my father does impresses me any more. Had Vesta curry and rice for dinner, during which Mrs. Singh came round and talked Hindi to Bert. She seemed to find our curry very funny, she kept pointing to it and laughing. Sometimes I think I am the only person in the world who still has manners.

Bert told my father that he is convinced the matron is trying to poison him (Bert, not my father), but my father said that all institutional food is the same. When it was time to go home, Bert started crying. He said, "Don't make me go back there," and other sad things. My father explained that we didn't have the skill to look after him at our house, so Bert was wheeled to the car (although he kept putting the brake of the wheelchair on). He asked us to keep his trunk at our house. He said it was to be opened on his death. The key is round his neck on a bit of string.

Dog is still AWOL.

Monday   October 12th
COLUMBUS DAY, USA. THANKSGIVING DAY, CANADA

Went to the "off-the-streets" youth club tonight. Rick
Lemon gave us a lecture on survival techniques. He
said that the best thing to do if you are suffering
from hypothermia is to climb into a plastic bag with
a naked woman. Pandora made a formal objection,
and Rick Lemon's girlfriend, Tit, got up and walked
away. It is just my luck to be on the mountain with a
frigid woman!

RIP Dog.

Tuesday   October 13th
FULL MOON

Had an angry phone call from my grandma to ask
when we were coming round to collect the dog! The
stupid dog turned up at her house on the 6th October. I went round immediately and was shocked at
the dog's condition: it looks old and gray. In human
years it is eleven years old. In dog years it should be
drawing a pension. I have never seen a dog age so
quickly. Those eight days with grandma must have
been hell. My grandma is very strict.

Wednesday   October 14th

I have nearly got used to the old ladies in the home
now. I call in every afternoon on my way home from
school. They seem pleased to see me. One of them is
knitting me a balaclava for my survival weekend.
She is called Queenie.

Did thirty-six and a half press-ups tonight.

Thursday   October 15th

Went to the youth club to try yukky, lousy old walking boots for size. Rick Lemon has hired them from a

mountaineering shop. To make mine fit I have to wear three pairs of socks. Six of us are going. Rick is leading us.

He is unqualified but experienced in surviving bad conditions. He was born and brought up in Kirkby New Town. I went to Sainsbury's and bought my survival food. We have got to carry our food and equipment in our rucksacks, so weight is an important factor. I bought:

1 box cornflakes
2 pints milk
box tea-bags
tin rhubarb
5 lb. spuds
½ lb. lard
½ lb. butter
2 loaves bread
1 lb. cheese
2 packets biscuits
2 lb. sugar
toilet roll
washing-up liquid
2 tins tuna
1 tin stewed steak
1 tin carrots

I could hardly carry my survival food home from Sainsbury's, so how I will manage it on a march across the hills I don't know! My father suggested leaving something out. So I have not packed the toilet roll or cornflakes.

Friday   October 16th

Have decided not to take my diary to Derbyshire. I cannot guarantee that it will not be read by hostile eyes. Besides it won't fit into my rucksack.

Must finish now, the mini-bus is outside papping its hooter.

Saturday   October 17th

Sunday   October 18th
EIGHTEENTH AFTER TRINITY

8 P.M. It is wonderful to be back in civilization!

I have lived like an ignoble savage for the past two days! Sleeping on rough ground with only a sleeping-bag between me and the elements! Trying to cook chips over a tiny primus stove! Trudging through streams in my torturous boots! Having to perform my natural functions out in the open! Wiping my bum on leaves! Not being able to have a bath or clean my teeth! No television or radio or anything! Rick Lemon wouldn't even let us sit in the mini-bus when it started to rain! He said we ought to make a shelter out of nature's bounty! Pandora found a plastic animal-food sack so we took it in turns sitting under it.

How I survived I don't know. My eggs broke, my bread got saturated, my biscuits got crushed and nobody had a tin-opener. I nearly starved. Thank God cheese doesn't leak, break, soak up water or come in a tin. I was glad when we were found and taken to the Mountain Rescue headquarters. Rick Lemon was told off for not having a map or compass. Rick said he knew the hills like the back of his hand. The chief mountain rescuer said that Rick must have been wearing gloves because we were seven miles from our mini-bus and heading in the wrong direction!

I shall now sleep in a bed for the first time in two days. No school tomorrow because of blisters.

Monday   October 19th

I have got to rest my feet for two days. Doctor Gray was very unpleasant: he said that he resented being called out for a few foot blisters.

I was very surprised at his attitude. It is a well-known fact that mountaineers get gangrene of the toes.

Tuesday   October 20th
MOON'S LAST QUARTER

Here I am lying in bed unable to walk because of excruciating pain and my father carries out his parental responsibilities by throwing a few bacon sandwiches at me three times a day!

If my mother doesn't come home soon I will end up deprived and maladjusted. I am already neglected.

Wednesday   October 21st

Hobbled to school. All the teachers were wearing their best clothes because it is Parents' Evening tonight. My father got cleaned up and put his best suit on. He looked OK, Thank God! Nobody could tell he was unemployed. My teachers all told him that I was a credit to the school.

Barry Kent's father was looking as sick as a pig. Ha! Ha! Ha!

Thursday   October 22nd

Limped half-way to school. Dog followed me. Limped back home. Shut dog in coal shed. Limped all the way to school. Fifteen minutes late. Mr. Scruton said it was not setting a good example for the late prefect to be late. It is all right for him to talk! He can ride to school in a Ford Cortina and then all he has to do is be in charge of a school. I have got a lot of problems and no car.

Friday   October 23rd

I have had a letter from the hospital to say that I have got to have my tonsils out on Tuesday the twenty-seventh. This has come as a complete shock to me! My father says I have been on the waiting list since I was five years old! So I have had to endure an annual bout of tonsillitis for nine years just because the National Health Service is starved of finance!

Why can't midwives remove babies' tonsils at birth? It would save a lot of trouble, pain and money.

Saturday   October 24th
UNITED NATIONS' DAY

Went shopping for new dressing gown, slippers, pyjamas, and toiletries. My father was moaning as usual. He said he didn't see why I couldn't just wear my old night-clothes in hospital. I told him that I would look ridiculous in my Peter Pan dressing gown and Winnie the Pooh pyjamas. Apart from the yukky design they are too small and covered in patches. He said that when he was a lad he slept in a nightshirt made out of two coal sacks stitched together. I phoned my grandma to check this suspicious statement and my father was forced to repeat it down the phone. My grandma said that they were not coal sacks but flour sacks, so I now know that my father is a pathological liar!

My hospital rig came to fifty-four pounds nineteen; this is before fruit, chocolates and Lucozade. Pandora said I looked like Noël Coward in my new bri-nylon dressing gown. I said, "Thanks, Pandora," although to be honest I don't know who Noël Coward is or was. I hope he's not a mass murderer or anything.

Sunday   October 25th
NINETEENTH AFTER TRINITY. BRITISH SUMMER TIME ENDS

Phoned my mother to tell her about my coming surgical ordeal. No reply. This is typical. She would sooner be out having fun with creep Lucas than comforting her only child!

Grandma rang and said that she knew somebody who knew somebody who knew somebody who had their tonsils out and bled to death on the operating theater table. She ended up by saying, "Don't worry Adrian, I'm sure everything will be all right for you."

Thanks a million, grandma!

Monday   October 26th
BANK HOLIDAY IN THE REP. OF IRELAND

11 A.M. I did my packing, then went to see Bert. He is sinking fast so it could be the last time we see each other. Bert also knows somebody who bled to death after a tonsils' extraction. I hope it's the same person.

Said goodbye to Pandora: she wept very touchingly. She brought me one of Blossom's old horseshoes to take into hospital. She said a friend of her father had a cyst removed and didn't come out of the anaesthetic. I'm being admitted to Ivy Swallow Ward at 2 P.M. Greenwich Mean Time.

6 P.M. My father has just left my bedside after four hours of waiting around for permission to leave. I have had every part of my body examined. Liquid substances have been taken from me, I have been weighed and bathed, measured and prodded and poked, but nobody has looked in my throat!

I have put our family medical dictionary on my bedside table so that the doctors see it and are impressed. I can't tell what the rest of the ward is like yet because the nurses have forgotten to remove the screens. A notice has been hung over my bed; it says "Liquids Only." I am dead scared.

10 P.M. I am starving! A black nurse has taken all my food and drink away. I am supposed to go to sleep but it is like bedlam in here. Old men keep falling out of bed.

Midnight. There is a new notice over my bed; it says "Nil by Mouth." I am dying of thirst! I would give my right arm for a can of Low Cal.

Tuesday   October 27th
NEW MOON

4 A.M. I am dehydrated!

6 A.M. Just been woken up! Operation is not until 10 A.M. So why couldn't they let me sleep? I have got to have another bath. I told them that it is the *inside* of my body that is being operated on, but they don't listen.

7 A.M. A Chinese nurse stayed in the bathroom to make sure I didn't drink any water. She kept staring so I had to put a hospital sponge over my thing.

7:30 A.M. I am dressed like a lunatic, ready for the operation. I have had an injection, it is supposed to make you sleepy but I'm wide awake listening to a row about a patient's lost notes.

8 A.M. My mouth is completely dry, I shall go mad from thirst, I haven't had a drink since nine forty-five last night, I feel very floaty, the cracks in the ceiling are very interesting. I have got to find somewhere to hide my diary. I don't want prying Nosy Parkers reading it.

8:30 A.M. My mother is at my bedside! She is going to put my diary in her organizer-handbag. She has promised (on the dog's life) not to read it.

8:45 A.M. My mother is in the hospital grounds smoking a cigarette. She is looking old and haggard. All the debauchery is catching up with her.

9 A.M. The operating trolley keeps coming into the ward and dumping unconscious men into beds. The trolley-pushers are wearing green overalls and wellingtons. There must be loads of blood on the floor of the theater!

9:15 A.M. The trolley is coming in my direction!

Midnight. I am devoid of tonsils. I am in a torrent of pain. It took my mother thirteen minutes to find my diary. She doesn't know her way round her organizer-handbag yet. It has got seventeen compartments.

Wednesday   October 28th

I am unable to speak. Even groaning causes agony.

Thursday   October 29th

I have been moved to a side ward. My suffering is too much for the other patients to bear.

Had a "get well" card from Bert and Sabre.

Friday   October 30th

I was able to sip a little of grandma's broth today. She brought it in her Thermos flask. My father brought me a family pack of crisps; he might just as well have brought me razor blades!

Pandora came at visiting time, I had little to whisper to her. Conversation palls when one is hovering between life and death.

Saturday   October 31st
HALLOWE'EN

3 A.M. I have been forced to complain about the noise coming from the nurses' home. I am sick of listening to (and watching) drunken nurses and off-duty policemen cavorting around the grounds dressed as witches and wizards. Nurse Boldry was doing something particularly unpleasant with a pumpkin.

I am joining BUPA as soon as they'll have me.

Sunday   November 1st
TWENTIETH AFTER TRINITY

The nurses have been very cold towards me. They say that I am taking up a bed that could be used by an ill person! I have got to eat a bowl of cornflakes before they let me out. So far I have refused; I cannot bear the pain.

Monday   November 2nd

Nurse Boldry forced a spoon of cornflakes down my damaged throat, then, before I could digest it, she started stripping my bed. She offered to pay for a taxi, but I told her that I would wait for my father to come and carry me out to the car.

Tuesday   November 3rd
ELECTION DAY, USA

I am in my own bed. Pandora is a tower of strength. She and I communicate without words. My voice has been damaged by the operation.

Wednesday   November 4th

Today I croaked my first words for a week. I said, "Dad, phone mum and tell her that I am over the worst." My father was overcome with relief and emotion. His laughter was close to hysteria.

Thursday   November 5th
MOON'S FIRST QUARTER

Dr. Gray says my malfunctioning voice is "only adolescent wobble." He is always in a bad mood!

He expected me to stagger to his surgery and queue in a germ-filled waiting room! He said I ought to be outside with other lads of my age building a bonfire. I told him that I was too old for such paganistic rituals. He said he was forty-seven and he still enjoyed a good burn-up.

Forty-seven! It explains a lot, he should be pensioned off.

Friday   November 6th

My father is taking me to an organized bonfire party tomorrow (providing I am up to it, of course). It is being held to raise funds for Marriage Guidance Councillors' expenses.

Pandora's mother is cooking the food and Pandora's father is in charge of the fireworks. My father is going to be in charge of lighting the bonfire so I'm going to stand at least a hundred meters away. I have seen him singe his eyebrows many times.

Last night some irresponsible people down our street had bonfire parties in their own back gardens! Yes!

In spite of being warned of all the dangers by the radio, television, *Blue Peter* and the media they went selfishly ahead. There were no accidents, but surely this was only luck.

Saturday   November 7th

The Marriage Guidance Council bonfire was massive. It was a good community effort. Mr. Cherry donated hundreds of copies of a magazine called *Now!* He said they had been cluttering up the back room of his shop for over a year.

Pandora burnt her collection of *Jackie* comics, she said that they "don't bear feminist analysis" and she "wouldn't like them to get into young girls' hands."

Mrs. Singh and all the little Singhs brought along

Indian firecrackers. They are much louder than English ones. I was glad our dog was locked in the coal shed with cotton wool in its ears.

Nobody was seriously burnt, but I think it was a mistake to hand out fireworks at the same time the food was being served.

I burnt the red phone bill that came this morning.

Sunday November 8th
TWENTY-FIRST AFTER TRINITY. REMEMBRANCE SUNDAY

Our street is full of acrid smoke. I went to see the bonfire, the *Now* magazines are still in the hot ashes, they are refusing to burn properly. (Our red phone bill has disappeared, thank God!)

Mr. Cherry is going to have to dig a big pit and pour quick-lime over the *Now* magazines before they choke the whole suburb.

Went to see Bert. He was out with Queenie.

Monday November 9th

Back to school. The dog is at the vet's having the cotton wool surgically removed.

Tuesday November 10th

My nipples have swollen! I am turning into a girl!!!

Wednesday November 11th
VETERANS' DAY, USA. REMEMBRANCE DAY, CANADA. FULL MOON

Dr. Gray has struck me off his list! He said nipple-swelling is common in boys. Usually they get it when they are twelve and a half. Dr. Gray said I was emotionally and physically immature! How can I be immature? I have had a rejection from the BBC! And how could I have walked to the surgery with swollen nipples?

I don't know why he calls it a surgery anyway; he never does any surgery in it.

Thursday   November 12th

Told Mr. Jones I couldn't do PE because of swollen nipples. He was extremely crude in his attitude. I don't know what they teach them at teacher-training college.

Friday   November 13th

Pandora and I had a frank talk about our relationship tonight. She doesn't want to marry me in two years' time!

She wants to have a career instead!

Naturally I am devastated by this blow. I told her I wouldn't mind her having a little job in a cake shop or something after our wedding, but she said she intended to go to university and that the only time she would enter a cake shop would be to buy a large crusty.

Harsh words were exchanged between us. (Hers were harsher than mine.)

Saturday   November 14th

Charred *Now!* magazines are blowing all over our cul-de-sac. They seem to have special powers of survival. The council have sent a special cleaning squad to try and trap them all.

The dog's ears are now clear of cotton wool. It only pretends not to hear.

Went to see B.B. but he is out with Queenie. She is pushing him around the leisure center.

Sunday   November 15th
TWENTY-SECOND AFTER TRINITY

Read *A Town Like Alice,* by Nevil Shute, it is dead brill. I wish I had an intellectual friend whom I could discuss great literature with. My father thinks *A Town Like Alice* was written by Lewis Carroll.

Monday   November 16th

I came home from school with a headache. All the noise and shouting and bullying is getting me down! Surely teachers should be better behaved!

Tuesday   November 17th

My father is a serious worry to me. Even the continuing news of Princess Diana's conception does not cheer him up.

Grandma has already knitted three pairs of bootees and sent them off care of Buckingham Palace. She is a true patriot.

Wednesday   November 18th
MOON'S LAST QUARTER

The trees are stark naked.
Their autumnal clothes
Litter the pavements.
Council sweepers apply fire
Thus creating municipal pyres.
I, Adrian Mole,
Kick them
And burn my Hush Puppies.

I have copied it out carefully and sent it to John Tydeman at the BBC. He strikes me as a man who might like poems about autumn leaves.

I have got to get something broadcast or printed soon else Pandora will lose all respect for me.

Thursday   November 19th

Pandora has suggested I start a literary magazine using the school duplicator. I wrote the first edition during dinner time. It is called *The Voice of Youth*.

Friday   November 20th

Pandora looked at *The Voice of Youth*. She suggested that instead of writing the whole magazine myself, I invite contributions from other talented scribblers.

She said she would do a piece about window-box gardening. Claire Neilson has submitted a punk poem, it is very avant garde, but I am not afraid to break new ground.

> *Punk Poem*
> Society is puke,
> Soiled vomit.
> On the Union Jack
> Sid was vicious
> Johnnie's rotten,
> Dead, dead, dead.
> Killed by grayness.
> England stinks.
> Sewer of the world.
> Cess-pit of Europe.
> Hail punks,
> Kings and Queens
> Of the street.

She wants it put in under an assumed name, her father is a Conservative councillor.

Nigel has written a short piece about racing-bike maintenance. It is very boring but I can't tell him because he is my best friend.

We go to press on Wednesday.

Pandora is typing the stencils over the weekend.

Here is my first editorial:

Hi Kids,
Well here's your very own school magazine. Yes!
Written and produced entirely using child labor.
I have tried to break new ground in our first edition. Many of you will be unaware of the miracles of window-box gardening and the joys of racing-bike maintenance. If so, hang on to your hats, you're in for a magic surprise!
ADRIAN MOLE, EDITOR

We are going to charge twenty-five pence a copy.

Saturday   November 21st

Pandora's father has stolen a box of stencils from his office. As I write, Pandora is typing the first pages of *The Voice of Youth.* I am half-way through writing an exposé about Barry Kent. It is called "Barry Kent: The Truth!" He hasn't dared to lay a finger on me since grandma's dramatic intervention, so I know I shall be safe.

Too busy to go and see Bert, I will go tomorrow.

Sunday   November 22nd
LAST AFTER TRINITY

Finished the exposé on Barry Kent. It will rock the school to its foundations. I have mentioned Barry Kent's sexual perversions—all about his disgusting practice of showing his thing for five pence a look.

Monday November 23rd

Had a Christmas card from grandma, and a letter from the post office to say that they are cutting the phone off!

Forgot to call round and see Bert. Pandora and I were too busy putting the paper to bed. How I wish I was putting Pandora to bed.

2 A.M. What am I going to do about the phone bill?

Tuesday November 24th

Nigel has just gone off in a sulk. He objected to the editing I did on his article. I tried to point out to him that one thousand five hundred words on bicycle spokes was pure self-indulgence, but he wouldn't listen. He has withdrawn his article. Thank God! Two pages less to fold.

The Voice of Youth hits the classrooms tomorrow. Must go and see Bert tomorrow.

Wednesday November 25th

We have been hit by a wildcat strike! Mrs. Clari-coates, the school secretary, has refused to handle *The Voice of Youth*. She says there is nothing in her job description to say she has to mess about with school magazines.

The editorial team offered to duplicate copies ourselves, but Mrs. Claricoates says that she alone knows how to "work the wretched thing." I am in despair. A whole six hours' work wasted!

Thursday November 26th
THANKSGIVING DAY, USA. NEW MOON

Pandora's father is photocopying *The Voice of Youth* on his office machine. He didn't want to, but Pandora sulked in her room and refused to eat until he agreed.

Friday   November 27th

Five hundred copies of *The Voice of Youth* were on sale in the dinner hall today.

Five hundred copies were locked in the games cupboard by the end of the afternoon. Not one copy was sold! Not one! My fellow pupils are nothing but Philistines and Morons!

We are dropping the price to twenty pence on Monday.

My mother phoned and wanted to speak to my father. I told her that he is on a fishing weekend with the Society of Redundant Electric Storage Heater Salesmen.

A postcard from the post office to say that unless my father phones the post office before five-thirty our phone will be disconnected.

Saturday   November 28th

A telegram! Addressed to me! The BBC? No, from my mother:

ADRIAN STOP COMING HOME STOP

What does she mean "Stop coming home"? How can I "stop coming home"? I live here.

The phone has been cut off! I am considering running away from home.

Sunday   November 29th
ADVENT SUNDAY

My mother has just turned up with no warning! She had all her suitcases with her. She has thrown herself on the mercy of my father. My father has just thrown himself on the body of my mother. I tactfully withdrew to my bedroom where I am now trying to work out how I feel about my mother's return. On the whole I am over the moon, but I'm dreading her looking around our squalid house. She will go mad when she finds out that I have lent Pandora her fox-fur coat.

Monday   November 30th
ST. ANDREW'S DAY

My mother and father were still in bed when I left for school.

Sold one copy of *The Voice of Youth,* to Barry Kent. He wanted to discover the truth about himself. He is a slow reader so it will probably take him until Friday to find out. We are going to try dropping the price to fifteen pence to try to stimulate demand. There are now four hundred and ninety-nine copies to be sold!

My mother and father are in bed again and its only 9 P.M.!

The dog is very pleased my mother is back. It has been going about smiling all day.

Tuesday   December 1st

I called the post office and pretended to be my father. I spoke in a very deep voice and told a lot of lies. I said that I, George Mole, had been in a lunatic asylum for three months and I needed the phone to ring up the Samaritans, etc. The woman sounded dead horrible, she said she was fed up with hearing lame excuses from irresponsible non-payers. She said that the phone would only be reconnected when £289.19 had been paid, plus £40 reconnection fee, plus a deposit of £40!

Three hundred and sixty-nine pounds! When my parents get out of bed and discover the lack of dialing tone, I will be done for!

Wednesday　December 2nd

My father tried to phone up after a job today! He has gone berserk.

My mother cleaned my bedroom, she turned up my mattress and found the *Big and Bouncy*s and the blue phone bill.

I sat on the kitchen stool while they interrogated me and shouted abuse. My father wanted to give me a "to-within-an-inch-of-his-life thrashing," but my mother stopped him. She said, "It would be more of a punishment to make the tight-fisted sod cough up some of his building-society savings." So that is what I'm being forced to do.

Now I will never be an owner-occupier.

Thursday　December 3rd

Drew out two hundred pounds from my building-society account. I don't mind admitting that there were tears in my eyes. It will take another fourteen years before I can replace it.

Friday　December 4th
MOON'S FIRST QUARTER

I am suffering from severe depression. It is all Pandora's father's fault. He should have had a holiday in England.

Saturday　December 5th

Had a letter from grandma to ask why I hadn't sent her a Christmas card yet.

Sunday　December 6th
SECOND IN ADVENT

I am still being treated like a criminal. My mother and father are not speaking to me, and I'm not allowed out. I might just as well turn to delinquency.

Monday   December 7th

Stole a Kevin Keegan key ring from Mr. Cherry's shop. It will do for Nigel's Christmas present.

Tuesday   December 8th

I am dead worried about the key ring; we did Morals and Ethics at school today.

Wednesday   December 9th

Can't sleep for worrying about the key ring. The papers are full of stories about old ladies getting done for shoplifting. I tried to overpay Mr. Cherry for my Mars bar, but he called me back and gave me my change.

Thursday   December 10th

Had a dream about a jailer locking me in a prison cell. The big iron key was attached to the Kevin Keegan key ring.
   The lousy, stinking, sodding phone is reconnected!

Friday   December 11th
FULL MOON

Phoned the Samaritans and confessed my crime. The man said, "Put it back then, lad." I will do it tomorrow.

Saturday   December 12th

Mr. Cherry caught me in the act of replacing the key ring. He has written a letter to my parents. I might as well do myself in.

Sunday   December 13th
THIRD IN ADVENT

Thank God there is no post on Sundays.

My mother and father had a festive time decorating the Christmas tree. I watched them hanging the baubles with a heavy heart.

I am reading *Crime and Punishment.* It is the most true book I have ever read.

Monday   December 14th

Got up at 5 A.M. to intercept the postman. Took the dog for a walk in the drizzle. (It wanted to stay asleep, but I wouldn't let it.) The dog moaned and complained all the way round the block so in the end I let it climb back into its cardboard box. I wish I was a dog; they haven't got any ethics or morals.

The postman delivered the letters at seven-thirty when I was sitting on the toilet. This is just my luck!

My father collected the letters and put them behind the clock. I had a quick look through them while he was coughing on his first cigarette of the day. Sure enough there was one addressed to my parents in Mr. Cherry's uneducated handwriting!

My mother and father slopped over each other for a few minutes and then opened the letters whilst their Rice Krispies were going soggy. There were seven lousy Christmas cards, which they put up on a string over the fireplace. My eyes were focused on Mr. Cherry's letter. My mother opened it, read it and said, "George, that old git Cherry's sent his bloody paper bill in." Then they ate their Rice Krispies and that was that. I wasted a lot of adrenalin worrying. I won't have enough left if I'm not careful.

Tuesday   December 15th

My mother has told me why she left creep Lucas and returned to my father. She said, "Bimbo treated me like a sex object, Adrian, and he expected his evening meal cooked for him, and he cut his toenails in the living room, and besides I'm very fond of your father." She didn't mention me.

Wednesday   December 16th

I am in an experimental Nativity play at school. It is called *Manger to Star*. I am playing Joseph. Pandora is playing Mary. Jesus is played by the smallest first-year. He is called Peter Brown. He is on drugs to make him taller.

Thursday   December 17th

Another letter from the BBC!

> Dear Adrian Mole,
> Thank you for submitting your latest poem. I understood it perfectly well once it had been typed. However, Adrian, understanding is not all. Our Poetry Department is inundated with Autumnal poems. The smell of bonfires and the crackling of leaves pervade the very corridors. Good try, but try again, eh?
> Yours with Best Wishes,
> John Tydeman

"Try again"! He is almost giving me a commission. I have written back to him:

> Dear Mr Tydeman,
> How much will I get if you broadcast one of my poems on the radio? When do you want me to send

it? What do you want it to be about? Can I read it out myself? Will you pay my train fare in advance? What time will it go out on the airways? I have to be in bed by ten.

Yours faithfully,

A. Mole

P.S. I hope you have a dead good Christmas.

Friday December 18th
MOON'S LAST QUARTER

Today's rehearsal of *Manger to Star* was a fiasco. Peter Brown has grown too big for the crib, so Mr. Animba, the Woodwork teacher, has got to make another one.

Mr. Scruton sat at the back of the gym and watched rehearsals. He had a face like the north face of the Eiger by the time we'd got to the bit where the three wise men were reviled as capitalist pigs.

He took Miss Elf into the showers and had a "Quiet Word." We all heard every word he shouted. He said he wanted to see a traditional Nativity play, with a Tiny Tears doll playing Jesus and three wise men dressed in dressing gowns and tea towels. He threatened to cancel the play if Mary, alias Pandora, continued to go into simulated labor in the manger. This is typical of Scruton, he is nothing but a small-minded, provincial, sexually-inhibited fascist pig. How he rose to become a headmaster I do not know. He has been wearing the same hairy green suit for three years. How can we change it all now? The play is being performed on Tuesday afternoon.

My mother has had a Christmas card from creep Lucas! Inside he had written, "Paulie, Have you got the dry-cleaning ticket for my best white suit? Sketchley's are being very difficult." My mother was very upset. My father rang Sheffield and ordered Lu-

cas to cease communications, or risk getting a bit of
Sheffield steel in between his porky shoulder blades.
My father looked dead good on the telephone. He had
a cigarette stuck between his lips. My mother was
leaning on the corner of the fridge. She had a cigarette in her hand. They looked a bit like the Hum-
phrey Bogart and Lauren Bacall postcard on my
wall. I wish I was a *real* gangster's son, at least you
would see a bit of life.

Saturday   December 19th

I've got no money for Christmas presents. But I have
made my Christmas list in case I find ten pounds in
the street.

   Pandora — Big bottle of Chanel No. 5 (£1.50)
   Mother — Egg-timer (75p)
   Father — Bookmark (38p)
   Grandma — Packet of J cloths (45p)
   Dog — Dog chocolates (45p)
   Bert — 20 Woodbines (95p)
   Auntie Susan — Tin of Nivea (60p)
   Sabre — Box of Bob Martins, small (39p)
   Nigel — Family box of Maltesers (34p)
   Miss Elf — Oven-glove (home-made)

Sunday   December 20th
FOURTH IN ADVENT

Pandora and I had a private Mary and Joseph re-
hearsal in my bedroom. We improvised a great scene
where Mary gets back from the Family Planning
Clinic and tells Joseph she's pregnant. I played
Joseph like Marlon Brando in *A Streetcar Named
Desire*. Pandora played Mary a bit like Blanche
Dubois; it was dead good until my father complained
about the shouting. The dog was supposed to be the

lowly cattle, but it wouldn't keep still long enough to
make a tableau.

After tea my mother casually mentioned that she
was going to wear her fox-fur coat to the school concert tomorrow. Shock! Horror! I immediately went
round to Pandora's house to get the mangy coat, only
to find that Pandora's mother has borrowed it to go
to the Marriage Guidance Christmas dinner and
dance! Pandora said that she hadn't realized that the
coat was only on loan; she thought it was a lover's
gift! How can a 14¾-year-old schoolboy afford to give
a fox-fur coat as a gift? Who does Pandora think I
am, a millionaire like Freddie Laker?

Pandora's mother won't be back until the early
hours so I will have to go round before school and
sneak the coat into its plastic cover. It's going to be
difficult, but then nothing in my life is simple or
straightforward any more. I feel like a character in a
Russian novel half the time.

Monday   December 21st

Woke up with a panic attack to see that it was eight-
fifty by my bedside digital! My black walls looked
unusually light and sparkly; one glance outside con-
firmed my suspicions that indeed the snow lay outside like a white carpet.

I stumbled through the snow to Pandora's house in
my father's fishing boots but found that the house
was devoid of humans. I looked through the letterbox and saw my mother's fur coat being mauled
about by Pandora's ginger cat. I shouted swear-
words at it but the lousy stinking cat just looked sar-
castic and carried on dragging the coat around the
hall. I had no choice but to shoulder-charge the
laundry room door and rush into the hall and rescue
my mother's coat. I left quickly (as quickly as anyone
can wearing thigh-length fishing boots, four sizes too

big). I put the fur coat on to keep me warm on my hazardous journey home. I nearly lost my bearings at the corner of Ploughman's Avenue and Shepherd's Crook Drive, but I fought my way through the blizzard until I saw the familiar sight of the prefabricated garages on the corner of our cul-de-sac.

I fell into our kitchen in a state of hypothermia and severe exhaustion; my mother was smoking a cigarette and making mince pies. She screamed, "What the bloody hell are you doing wearing my fox-fur coat?" She was not kind or concerned or anything that mothers are supposed to be. She fussed about, wiping snow off the coat and drying the fur with a hair dryer. She didn't even offer to make me a hot drink or anything. She said, "It's been on the radio that the school is closed because of the snow, so you can make yourself useful and check the camp beds for rust. The Sugdens are staying over Christmas." The Sugdens! My mother's relations from Norfolk! Yuk, Yuk. They are all inbred and can't speak properly!

Phoned Pandora to explain about the fox fur and the damage, etc., but she had gone skiing on the slope behind the Co-op bakery. Pandora's father asked me to get off the line, he had to make an urgent phone call to the police station. He said he had just come home and discovered a break-in! He said the place was a shambles (the cat must have done it, I was very careful), but fortunately the only thing that was missing was an old fox-fur coat that Pandora had lined the cat's basket with.

Sorry, Pandora, but this is the final straw that broke the donkey's back! You can find yourself another Joseph, I refuse to share the stage with a girl who puts her cat's comfort before her boyfriend's dilemma.

Tuesday   December 22nd

School was closed this morning because the teachers couldn't manage to get in on time because of the snow. That will teach them to live in old mill houses and windmills out in the country! Miss Elf lives with a West Indian in a terraced house in the town, so she bravely turned out to prepare for the school concert in the afternoon. I decided to forgive Pandora for the fox fur in the cat's basket incident after she had pointed out that the cat was an expectant mother.

The school concert was not a success. The bell ringing from class One-G went on too long, my father said "The Bells! The Bells!" and my mother laughed too loudly and made Mr. Scruton look at her.

The school orchestra was a disaster! My mother said, "When are they going to stop tuning-up and start playing?" I told her that they had just played a Mozart horn concerto. That made my mother and father and Pandora's mother and father start laughing in a very unmannerly fashion. When ten-stone Alice Bernard from Three-C came on stage in a tutu and did the dying swan I thought my mother would explode. Alice Bernard's mother led the applause, but not many people followed.

The Dumbo class got up and sang a few boring old carols. Barry Kent sang all the vulgar versions (I know because I was watching his lips) then they sat down cross-legged, and brain-box Henderson from Five-K played a trumpet, Jew's harp, piano and guitar. The smarmy git looked dead superior when he was bowing during his applause. Then it was the interval and time for me to change into my white T-shirt-and-Wranglers Joseph costume. The tension backstage was electric. I stood in the wings (a theatrical term—it means the side of the stage) and watched the audience filing back into their places.

Then the music from *Close Encounters* boomed out over the stereo speakers, and the curtains opened on an abstract manger and I just had time to whisper to Pandora "Break a leg, darling," before Miss Elf pushed us out into the lights. My performance was brilliant! I really got under the skin of Joseph but Pandora was less good, she forgot to look tenderly at Jesus/Peter Brown.

The three punks/wise men made too much noise with their chains and spoiled my speech about the Middle East situation, and the angels representing Mrs. Thatcher got hissed by the audience so loudly that their spoken chorus about unemployment was wasted.

Still, all in all, it was well received by the audience. Mr. Scruton got up and made a hypocritical speech about "a brave experiment" and "Miss Elf's tireless work behind the scenes," and then we all sang "We wish you a Merry Christmas!"

Driving home in the car my father said, "That was the funniest Nativity play I have ever seen. Whose idea was it to turn it into a comedy?" I didn't reply. It wasn't a comedy.

Wednesday   December 23rd

9 A.M. Only two shopping days left for Christmas and I am still penniless. I have made a Blue Peter oven-glove for Miss Elf, but in order to give it to her in time for Christmas I will have to go into the ghetto and risk getting mugged.

I will have to go out carol singing, there is nothing else I can do to raise finances.

10 P.M. Just got back from carol singing. The suburban houses were a dead loss. People shouted, "Come back at Christmas," without even opening the door. My most appreciative audience were the drunks staggering in and out of the Black Bull. Some of them wept openly at the beauty of my solo rendition of "Silent Night." I must say that I presented a touching picture as I stood in the snow with my young face lifted to the heavens ignoring the scenes of drunken revelry around me.

I made £3.13½ plus an Irish tenpence and a Guinness bottletop. I'm going out again tomorrow. I will wear my school uniform, it should be worth a few extra quid.

Thursday   December 24th

Took Bert's Woodbines round to the home. Bert is hurt because I haven't been to see him. He said he didn't want to spend Christmas with a lot of malicious old women. Him and Queenie are causing a scandal. They are unofficially engaged. They have got their names on the same ashtray. I have invited Bert and Queenie for Christmas Day. My mother doesn't know yet but I'm sure she won't mind, we have got a big turkey. I sang a few carols for the old ladies. I made two pounds eleven pence out of them so I went to Woolworth's to buy Pandora's Chanel No. 5. They hadn't got any so I bought her an underarm deodorant instead.

The house looks dead clean and sparkling, there is a magic smell of cooking and satsumas in the air. I have searched around for my presents but they are not in the usual places. I want a racing bike, nothing else will please me. It's time I was independently mobile.

11 P.M. Just got back from the Black Bull. Pandora came with me, we wore our school uniforms and reminded all the drunks of their own children. They coughed up conscience money to the tune of twelve pounds fifty-seven! So we are going to see a pantomime on Boxing Day and we will have a family bar of Cadbury's Dairy Milk each!

Friday   December 25th
CHRISTMAS DAY

Got up at 5 A.M. to have a ride on my racing bike. My father paid for it with American Express. I couldn't ride it far because of the snow, but it didn't matter. I just like looking at it. My father had written on the gift tag attached to the handlebars, "Don't leave it out in the rain this time"—as if I would!

My parents had severe hangovers, so I took them breakfast in bed and gave them my presents at the same time. My mother was overjoyed with her egg-timer and my father was equally delighted with his bookmark, in fact everything was going OK until I casually mentioned that Bert and Queenie were my guests for the day, and would my father mind getting out of bed and picking them up in his car.

The row went on until the lousy Sugdens arrived. My grandma and grandad Sugden and Uncle Dennis and his wife Marcia and their son Maurice all look the same, as if they went to funerals every day of their lives. I can hardly believe that my mother is related to them. The Sugdens refused a drink and had a cup of tea whilst my mother defrosted the turkey in the bath. I helped my father carry Queenie (fifteen stone) and Bert (fourteen stone) out of our car. Queenie is one of those loud types of old ladies who dye their hair and try to look younger. Bert is in love with her. He told me when I was helping him into the toilet.

Grandma Mole and Auntie Susan came at twelve-thirty and pretended to like the Sugdens. Auntie Susan told some amusing stories about life in prison but nobody but me and my father and Bert and Queenie laughed.

I went up to the bathroom and found my mother crying and running the turkey under the hot tap.

She said, "The bloody thing won't thaw out, Adrian. What am I going to do?" I said, "Just bung it in the oven." So she did.

We sat down to eat Christmas dinner four hours late. By then my father was too drunk to eat anything. The Sugdens enjoyed the Queen's Speech but nothing else seemed to please them. Grandma Sugden gave me a book called *Bible Stories for Boys*. I could hardly tell her that I had lost my faith, so I said thank-you and wore a false smile for so long that it hurt.

The Sugdens went to their camp beds at ten o'clock. Bert, Queenie and my mother and father played cards while I polished my bike. We all had a good time making jokes about the Sugdens. Then my father drove Bert and Queenie back to the home and I phoned Pandora up and told her that I loved her more than life itself.

I am going round to her house tomorrow to give her the deodorant and escort her to the pantomime.

Saturday December 26th
BANK HOLIDAY IN UK AND REP. OF IRELAND (a day may be given in lieu). NEW MOON

The Sugdens got up at 7 A.M. and sat around in their best clothes looking respectable. I went out on my bike. When I got back my mother was still in bed, and my father was arguing with Grandad Sugden about our dog's behavior, so I went for another ride.

I called in on Grandma Mole, ate four mince pies, then rode back home. I got up to 30 mph on the dual carriageway, it was dead good. I put my new suede jacket and corduroy trousers on (courtesy of my father's Barclaycard) and called for Pandora; she gave me a bottle of after-shave for my Christmas present. It was a proud moment, it signified the *End of Childhood.*

We quite enjoyed the pantomime but it was rather childish for our taste. Bill Ash and Carole Hayman were good as Aladdin and the Princess, but the robbers played by Jeff Teare and Ian Giles were best. Sue Pomeroy gave a hilarious performance as Widow Twankey. In this she was greatly helped by her cow, played by Chris Martin and Lou Wakefield.

Sunday   December 27th
IST AFTER CHRISTMAS

The Sugdens have gone back to Norfolk, thank God!

The house is back to its usual mess. My parents took a bottle of vodka and two glasses to bed with them last night. I haven't seen them since.

Went to Melton Mowbray on my bike, did it in five hours.

Monday   December 28th

I am in trouble for leaving my bike outside last night. My parents are not speaking to me. I don't care, I have just had a shave and I feel magic.

Tuesday   December 29th

My father is in a bad mood because there is only a bottle of V.P. sherry left to drink. He has gone round Pandora's house to borrow a bottle of spirits.

The dog has pulled the Christmas tree down and made all the pine needles stick in the shag-pile.

I have finished all my Christmas books and the library is still shut. I am reduced to reading my father's *Reader's Digests* and testing my word power.

Wednesday   December 30th

All the balloons have shriveled up. They look like old women's breasts shown on television documentaries about the Third World.

Thursday   December 31st

The last day of the year! A lot has happened. I have fallen in love. Been a one-parent child. Gone Intellectual. And had two letters from the BBC. Not bad going for a 14¾ year old!

My mother and father have been to a New Year's Eve dance at the Grand Hotel. My mother actually wore a dress! It is over a year since she showed her legs in public.

Pandora and I saw the New Year in together, we had a dead passionate session accompanied by Andy Steward and a bagpiper.

My father came crashing through the front door at 1 A.M. carrying a lump of coal in his hand. Drunk as usual.

My mother started going on about what a wonderful son I was and how much she loved me. It's a pity she never says anything like that when she is sober.

Friday January 1st
BANK HOLIDAY IN UK, REP. OF IRELAND, USA AND CANADA

These are my New Year's resolutions:

1. I will be true to Pandora.
2. I will bring my bike in at night.
3. I will not read unworthy books.
4. I will study hard for my O levels, and get Grade A's.
5. I will try to be more kind to the dog.
6. I will try to find it in my heart to forgive Barry Kent his multiple sins.
7. I will clean the bath after use.
8. I will stop worrying about the size of my thing.
9. I will do my back-stretching exercises every night without fail.
10. I will learn a new word and use it every day.

Saturday January 2nd
BANK HOLIDAY IN SCOTLAND (a day may be given in lieu)

How interesting it is that Aabec should be an Australian bark used for making sweat.

Sunday January 3rd
SECOND AFTER CHRISTMAS. MOON'S FIRST QUARTER

I wouldn't mind going to Africa and hunting an Aardvark.

Monday January 4th

Whilst in Africa I would go South and look out for an Aardwolf.

Tuesday January 5th

And I would avoid tangling with an Aasvogel.

Wednesday January 6th
EPIPHANY

I keep having nightmares about the bomb. I hope it isn't dropped before I get my GCE results in August 1982. I wouldn't like to die an unqualified virgin.

Thursday January 7th

Nigel came round to look at my racing bike. He said that it was mass produced, unlike his bike that was "made by a craftsman in Nottingham." I have gone off Nigel, and I have also gone off my bike a bit.

Friday January 8th

Got a wedding invitation from Bert and Queenie, they are getting married on January 16th at Pocklington Street Register Office.

In my opinion it is a waste of time. Bert is nearly ninety and Queenie is nearly eighty. I will leave it until the last minute before I buy a wedding present.

It has started snowing again. I asked my mother to buy me some green wellingtons like the Queen's but she came back with dead common black ones. I only need them to walk Pandora to our gate. I am staying in until the snow melts. Unlike most youths of my age, I dislike frolicking in the snow.

Saturday January 9th
FULL MOON

Nigel said the end of the world is coming tonight. He said the moon is having a total collapse. (Nigel should read *Reader's Digest* and increase his word power.) True enough it did go dark, I held my breath and feared the worst but then the moon recovered and life went on as usual, except in York where fate has flooded the town center.

Sunday January 10th
FIRST AFTER EPIPHANY

I can't understand why my father looks so old at forty-one compared to President Reagan at seventy. My father has got no work or worries yet he looks dead haggard. Poor President Reagan has to carry the world's safety on his shoulders yet he is always smiling and looking cheerful. It doesn't make sense.

Monday January 11th

I've been looking through last year's diary and have been reminded that Malcolm Muggeridge never did reply to my letter about what to do if you are an intellectual. That is a first-class stamp wasted! I should have written to the British Museum, that's where all the intellectuals hang out.

Tuesday January 12th

Pandora and I went to the youth club tonight. It was quite good. Rick Lemon led a discussion on sex. Nobody said anything, but he showed some interesting slides of wombs cut in half.

Wednesday January 13th

Pandora's parents have had a massive row. They are sleeping in separate bedrooms. Pandora's mother has joined the SDP and Pandora's father is staying loyal to the Labor Party.

Pandora is a Liberal, so she gets on all right with them both.

Thursday   January 14th

Pandora's father has come out of the closet and admitted that he is a Bennite. Pandora is staying loyal to him, but if the Co-op Dairy find out he will be finished.

Friday   January 15th

Thank God the snow is melting! At last I can walk the streets in safety, secure in the knowledge that no one is going to ram a snowball down the back of my anorak.

Saturday   January 16th
MOON'S LAST QUARTER

Bert got married today.

The Alderman Cooper Sunshine Home hired a coach and took the old ladies to form a guard of honor with their walking-frames.

Bert looked dead good. He cashed his life insurance in and spent the money on a new suit. Queenie was wearing a hat made of flowers and fruit. She had a lot of orange make-up on her face to try and cover the wrinkles. Even Sabre had a red bow round his neck. I think it was kind of the RSPCA to let Sabre out for his master's wedding. My father and Pandora's father carried Bert's wheelchair up the steps with Bert a single man and then down again with Bert a married man. The old ladies threw rice and confetti and my mother and Pandora's mother gave Queenie a kiss and a lucky horseshoe.

A newspaper reporter and photographer made everyone pose for photographs. I was asked my name, but I said I didn't want publicity for my acts of charity to Bert.

The reception took place back at the home. Ma-

tron made a cake with *B* and *Q* written in Jelly-
tots.

Bert and Queenie are moving into a bungalow on
Monday, after they have had their honeymoon in the
home.

Honeymoon! Ha! Ha! Ha!

Sunday   January 17th
SECOND AFTER EPIPHANY

Last night I dreamed about a boy like me collecting
pebbles in the rain. It was a dead strange dream.

I am reading *The Black Prince,* by Iris Murdoch. I
can only understand one word in ten. It is now my
ambition to actually enjoy one of her books. Then I
will know I am above the common herd.

Monday   January 18th

School. First day of term. Loads of GCE homework. I
will never cope. I am an intellectual but at the same
time I am not very clever.

Tuesday   January 19th

Brought four hundred and eighty three copies of *The
Voice of Youth* home in my satchel and Adidas bag.
Mr. Jones needs the games cupboard.

Wednesday   January 20th

Two-and-a-half hours of homework! I will crack under the strain.

Thursday   January 21st

My brain is hurting. I have just had two pages of
Macbeth to translate into English.

Friday   January 22nd

I am destined to become a manual worker. I can't keep working under this pressure. Miss Elf said my work is perfectly satisfactory, but that isn't good enough when Pandora keeps getting "Excellent" in red pen on everything she does.

Saturday   January 23rd

Stayed in bed until five-thirty to make sure I missed Sainsbury's. Listened to Radio Four play about domestic unhappiness. Phoned Pandora. Did Geography homework. Teased dog. Went to sleep. Woke up. Worried for ten minutes. Got up. Made cocoa.

I am a nervous wreck.

Sunday   January 24th
THIRD AFTER EPIPHANY

My mother blames my bad nerves on Iris Murdoch. She says painful adolescence shouldn't be read about when one is studying for O levels.

Monday   January 25th
NEW MOON

Couldn't do my Math homework. Phoned the Samaritans. The nice man on the end of the phone told me the answer was nine-eighths. He was dead kind to someone in despair.

Tuesday   January 26th

The stupid Samaritan got the answer wrong! It's only seven-fifths. I only got six out of twenty. Pandora got them all right. In fact she got a hundred percent.

Wednesday   January 27th

My mother is holding her woman's rights meetings in our lounge. I can't concentrate on my homework properly with women laughing and shouting and stamping up the stairs. They are not a bit lady-like.

Thursday   January 28th

Got fifteen out of twenty for History. Pandora got twenty-one out of twenty. She got an extra mark for knowing Hitler's father's name.

Friday   January 29th

Came home from school early with a severe migraine (missed the Comparative Religion test). Found my father watching *Play School* and pretending to be an acorn growing into an oak.

   Went to bed too shocked to speak.

Saturday   January 30th

Migraine. Too ill to write.

Sunday   January 31st
FOURTH AFTER EPIPHANY

Pandora came round. I copied her homework. Feel better.

Monday   February 1st
MOON'S FIRST QUARTER

My mother has given my father an ultimatum: either he finds a job, or starts doing housework, or leaves.

   He is looking for a job.

Tuesday   February 2nd
CANDLEMAS (SCOTTISH QUARTER-DAY)

Grandma Mole came round to tell me that the end of
the world was announced at her Spiritualist church
last week. She said it should have all ended yesterday.

She would have come round sooner only she was
washing her curtains.

Wednesday   February 3rd

My father has had his credit cards taken off him!
Barclays, Nat West and American Express have got
fed up with his reckless spending. Time is running
out for us. He has only got a few quids' redundancy
money left in his sock drawer.

My mother is looking for a job.

I have got a sense of *déjà vu.*

Thursday   February 4th

Went round to see Bert and Queenie. Their bungalow is so full of knick-knacks that there is hardly
room for a person to move. Sabre knocks at least ten
things over every time he wags his tail. They both
seem happy enough, though their sex life can't be up
to much.

Friday   February 5th

I've got to write an essay on the causes of the Second
World War. What a waste of time! Everyone knows
the causes. You can't go anywhere without seeing
Hitler's photo.

Saturday   February 6th

Finished essay; copied it out of *Pear's Encylopedia.*

My mother has gone to a woman's workshop on

self-defense. So if my father moans at her for burning the toast she will be able to karate-chop him in the windpipe.

Sunday   February 7th
SEPTUAGESIMA

Bored stiff all day. My parents never do anything on Sundays but read the Sunday papers. Other families go out to safari parks, etc. But we never do.

When I am a parent I will fill my children with stimulation at weekends.

Monday   February 8th
FULL MOON

My mother has found a job. She collects money from Space Invader machines. She started today in response to an urgent phone call from the job agency that she is registered with.

She said that the fullest machines are those in unrespectable cafés and university common rooms.

I think my mother is betraying her principles. She is pandering to an obsession of weak minds.

Tuesday   February 9th

My mother has given up her job. She said she is sexually harassed during her work and she is also allergic to ten-pence pieces.

Wednesday   February 10th

My father is going to start his own business making spice-racks. He has spent the last of his redundancy money on buying pine and glue. Our spare bedroom has been turned into a workshop. Sawdust is all over the house.

I am very proud of my father. He is now a company director, and I am a company director's son!

Thursday   February 11th

Delivered Mrs. Singh's massive spice-rack after school. It took two of us to carry it round and install it on her kitchen wall. We had a cup of sickly Indian tea and Mrs. Singh paid my father and then started to fill up her shelves with exotic Indian spices. They looked a lot more interesting than my mother's boring parsley and thyme.

My father bought a bottle of champagne to celebrate his first sale! He has got no respect for capital investment.

Friday   February 12th

Pandora has gone to London with her father to hear Tony Benn speak. Pandora's mother has gone to a SDP rally in Loughborough. It is a sad day when families are split asunder by politics.

I'm not sure how I will vote. Sometimes I think Mrs. Thatcher is a nice kind sort of woman. Then the next day I see her on television and she frightens me rigid. She has got eyes like a psychotic killer, but a voice like a gentle person. It is a bit confusing.

Saturday   February 13th

Pandora has got a crush on Tony Benn, just like the one she had on Adam Ant. She says that older men are exciting.

I am trying to grow my mustache. Valentine's Day tomorrow. A big card came today, it had a Sheffield postmark.

Sunday February 14th
SEXAGESIMA. ST. VALENTINE'S DAY

At last I have had a valentine from somebody who is
not a blood relation! Pandora's card was charming,
she had written a simple message of love:
    Adrian, it is you alone.
I gave Pandora a false Victorian card, inside I wrote:

    My young love,
    Treacle hair and knee-socks
    Give my system deep shocks.
    You've got a magic figure:
    I'm Roy Rogers, you are Trigger.

It doesn't scan very well, but I was in a hurry. Pandora didn't get the literary reference to Roy Rogers,
so I have lent her my father's old Roy Rogers annuals.
    My father threw the Sheffield card in the waste
bin. My mother took it out when my father had gone
to the pub. Inside it said:
    Pauline, I am in anguish.
My mother smiled and ripped it up.

Monday February 15th
WASHINGTON'S BIRTHDAY, USA. MOON'S LAST QUARTER

Came home from school to hear my mother talking
to creep Lucas on the phone. She was using a yukky
voice and saying things like: "Don't ask me to do it,
Bimbo," and "It's all over between us now, darling.
We must try to forget."
    I can't stand much more emotional stress. I am up
to my ears in it already what with studying hard and
vying with Tony Benn for Pandora's attention.

Tuesday   February 16th

Pandora's mother came round last night to complain about her spice-rack. It fell off the wall and spilt rosemary and tumeric all over her cork tiles. My mother apologized on behalf of my father who was hiding in the coal shed.

I am seriously thinking of giving everything up and running away to be a tramp. I would quite enjoy the life, providing I could have a daily bath.

Wednesday   February 17th

Miss Elf told us about her boyfriend today. He is called Winston Johnson. He is a Master of Arts and can't get a job! So what chance do I stand?

Miss Elf said that school-leavers are despairing all over the country. She said that Mr. Scruton should be ashamed to have a portrait of Mrs. Thatcher over his desk.

I think I am turning radical.

Thursday   February 18th

This morning the whole school was ordered to go to the assembly hall. Mr. Scruton got up on the stage and acted like the films of Hitler. He said in all his long years of teaching he had never come across an act of such serious vandalism. Everybody went dead quiet and wondered what had happened. Scruton said that somebody had entered his office and drawn a mustache on Margaret Thatcher and written "Three million unemployed" in her cleavage.

He said that defiling the greatest leader this country has ever known was a crime against humanity. It was tantamount to treason and that when the culprit was found they would be immediately expelled. Scruton's eyes bulged out so far that a few of the first-years started to cry. Miss Elf led them outside to safety.

The whole school has got to have handwriting tests.

Friday   February 19th

Miss Elf has resigned. I will miss her, she was responsible for my political development. I am a committed radical. I am against nearly everything.

Saturday   February 20th

Pandora, Nigel, Claire Neilson and myself have formed a radical group. We are the "Pink Brigade." We discuss things like war (we are against it); peace (we are for it); and the ultimate destruction of capitalist society.

Claire Neilson's father is a capitalist: he owns a greengrocer's shop. Claire is trying to get her father to give cheap food to the unwaged but he refuses. He waxes fat on their starvation!

Sunday   February 21st
QUINQUAGESIMA

Had an argument with my father over the *Sunday Express*. He can't see that he is a willing tool of the reactionary right. He refuses to change to the *Morning Star*. My mother reads anything; she is prostituting her literacy.

Monday   February 22nd

Once again I am spotty. I am also extremely sexually frustrated. I'm sure a session of passionate lovemaking would improve my skin.

Pandora says she is not going to risk being a single parent just for the sake of a few spots. So I will have to fall back on self-indulgence.

Tuesday   February 23rd
SHROVE TUESDAY. NEW MOON

Ate nine pancakes at home, three at Pandora's and four at Bert and Queenie's. Grandma was very hurt when I refused her kind offer to whip me a batter, but I was full up.

It is disgusting when the Third World is living on a few grains of rice.

I feel dead guilty.

Wednesday   February 24th
ASH WEDNESDAY

Our school dinner-ladies have got the sack! The dinners now come in hot boxes from a central kitchen. I would have staged a protest but I have got a Geography test tomorrow.

Mrs. Leech was presented with a microwave oven for her thirty years of toil over the custard jug.

Thursday   February 25th

Got fifteen out of twenty for Geography. I lost points for saying that the Falkland Islands belonged to Argentina.

Friday   February 26th

My thing is now thirteen centimeters long when it is extended. When it is contracted it is hardly worth measuring. My general physique is improving. I think the back-stretching exercises are paying off. I used to be the sort of boy who had sand kicked in his face, now I'm the sort of boy who watches somebody else have it kicked in their face.

Saturday   February 27th

My father hasn't made or sold a single spice-rack all
week. We are now living on Social Security and dole
money.

My mother has stopped smoking. The dog is down
to half a tin of Chum a day.

Sunday   February 28th
QUADRAGESIMA (FIRST IN LENT)

Had egg and chips and peas for Sunday dinner! No
pudding! Not even a proper serviette.

My mother says we are the *nouveau poor*.

Monday   March 1st
ST. DAVID'S DAY (WALES)

My father has stopped smoking. He is going around
with a white face finding fault with everything I
do.

My mother and him had their first row since she
came back. The dog caused it by eating the Spam
for tea. It couldn't help it, the poor thing was half
crazed with hunger. It is back on a full tin of Chum
a day.

Tuesday   March 2nd
MOON'S FIRST QUARTER

My parents are suffering severe nicotine withdrawal
symptoms. It is quite amusing to a non-smoker like
me.

Wednesday   March 3rd

I had to lend my father enough money for a gallon of
petrol, he had an interview for a job. My mother cut
his hair and gave him a shave and told him what to
say and how to behave. It is pathetic to see how

unemployment has reduced my father to childish dependence on others.

He is waiting to hear from Manpower Services.

He is still ill from not smoking. His temper has reached new peaks of explosion.

Thursday   March 4th

No news yet about the job. I spend as much time as I can out of the house. My parents are unbearable. I almost wish they would start smoking again.

Friday   March 5th

He got it!!!

He starts on Monday as a Canal Bank Renovation Supervisor. He is in charge of a gang of schoolleavers. To celebrate he bought my mother sixty Benson and Hedges and himself sixty Players. I got a family pack of Mars bars.

Everybody is dead happy for once. Even the dog has cheered up a bit. Grandma is knitting my father a woolly hat for work.

Saturday   March 6th

Pandora and I went to see the bit of canal bank that my father is now in charge of. If he worked for a thousand years he will never get it cleaned of all the old bikes and prams and weeds and Coca Cola tins! I told my father that he was in a no-win situation, but he said, "On the contrary, in one year's time it will be a beauty spot." Yes! And I am Nancy Reagan, Dad!

Sunday   March 7th
SECOND IN LENT

My father went to see his canal bank this morning. He came home and shut himself in his bedroom. He is still there, I can hear my mother saying encouraging words to him.

It is uncertain whether or not he will turn up for work tomorrow. On the whole I think not.

Monday   March 8th

He went to work.

After school I walked home along the canal bank. I found him bossing a gang of skinheads and punks about. They were looking surly and uncooperative. None of them wanted to get their clothes dirty. My father seemed to be the only one doing any work. He was covered in mud. I attempted to exchange a few civilities with the lads, but they spurned my overtures. I pointed out that the lads are alienated by a cruel, uncaring society, but my father said, "Bugger off home, Adrian. You're talking a load of lefty crap." He will have a mutiny on his hands soon if he's not careful.

Tuesday   March 9th
FULL MOON

My schoolwork is plummeting down to new depths. I only got five out of twenty for spelling. I think I might be anorexic.

Wednesday   March 10th

My father has asked me not to bring Pandora to the canal after school. He says he can't do anything with the lads after she has gone. It's true that she is stunningly beautiful, but the lads will just have to learn self-control. I have had to learn it. She has refused to consummate our relationship. Sometimes I wonder what she sees in me.

I live in daily terror of our relationship ending.

Thursday   March 11th

Pandora and Pandora's mother have joined my mother's woman's group. No men or boys are allowed in our front room. My father had to be in charge of the crêche in our dining room.

Rick Lemon's baby daughter Herod was crawling under the table shouting: "Tit! Tit!" My father kept telling Herod to shut up until I explained that Tit was Herod's mother's name. Herod is a very radical baby who never eats sweets and stays up until 2 A.M.

My father says that women ought to be at home cooking. He said it in a whisper so that he wouldn't be karate-chopped to death.

Friday   March 12th

My father had a good day on the canal bank. He is almost through to the grass now. To celebrate he brought the skinheads and punks round to our house for a glass of home-made beer. Mrs. Singh and my mother looked shocked when the lads trooped into our kitchen, but my father introduced Baz, Daz, Maz, Kev, Melv and Boz and my mother and Mrs. Singh relaxed a bit.

Boz is going to help me fix the brakes on my bike, he is an expert bike-fixer. He has been stealing them since he was six.

Saturday   March 13th

Boz offered me a sniff of his glue today, but I declined it with thanks.

Sunday   March 14th
THIRD IN LENT

All the women I know have gone to rally to protest about a woman's right to work. Mrs. Singh has gone wearing a disguise.

Saw Rick Lemon on the park, he was pushing Herod too high on a swing. Herod was shouting: "Tit! Tit!"

Monday   March 15th

I am loved by two women! Elizabeth Sally Broadway gave Victoria Louise Thomson a note in Science. It said: "Ask Adrian Mole if he wants to go out with me."

Victoria Louise Thomson (hereafter known as V.L.T.) passed on the message. I replied to V.L.T. in the negative.

Elizabeth Sally Broadway (hereafter known as E.S.B.) looked dead sad and started to cry into her bunsen burner.

It is really wonderful to know that Pandora and Elizabeth are both in love with me.

Perhaps I am not so ugly after all.

Tuesday   March 16th

Pandora and E.S.B. have had a fight in the playground. I am disgusted with Pandora. At the last meeting of the Pink Brigade she swore to be a pacifist all her life.

Pandora won! Ha! Ha! Ha!

Wednesday   March 17th
ST. PATRICK'S DAY. BANK HOLIDAY (IRELAND). MOON'S LAST QUARTER

Mr. O'Leary was brought home by a police car at 10.30 P.M. Mrs. O'Leary came over to ask my father if he would help her to get Mr. O'Leary upstairs to bed. My father is still over there. I can hear the music and singing through my double-glazing.

It is no joke when you need your sleep for school.

Thursday   March 18th

I am reading *How Children Fail,* by John Holt. It is
dead good. If I fail my O levels it will be all my parents' fault.

Friday   March 19th

My creative English essay:

Spring, by A Mole
The trees explode into bud, indeed some of them
are in leaf. Their branches thrust to the sky like
drunken scarecrows. Their trunks writhe and
twist into the earth and form a plethora of roots.
The brilliant sky hovers uncertainly like a shy
bride at the door of her nuptial chamber. Birds
wing and scrape their erratic way into the cotton-
wool clouds like drunken scarecrows. The translucent brook gurgles majestically towards its journey's end. "To the sea!" it cries, "to the sea!" it
endlessly repeats.
    A lonely boy, his loins afire, sits and watches his
calm reflection in the torrential brook. His heart is
indeed heavy. His eyes fall on to the ground and
rest on a wondrous majestic many-hued butterfly.
The winged insect takes flight and the boy's eyes
are carried far away until they are but a speck on
the red-hued sunset. He senses on the zephyr a
hope for mankind.

Pandora thinks this is the best thing I have ever
written, but I know I have got a long way to go until I
have learned my craft.

Saturday   March 20th
VERNAL EQUINOX

My mother has had all her hair cut off. She looks like one of Auntie Susan's inmates. She doesn't look a bit maternal any more. I don't know whether to get her anything for Mother's Day or not. She was going on about it last night, saying it was a commercial racket fed by gullible fools.

Sunday   March 21st
FOURTH IN LENT. MOTHERING SUNDAY

11:30 A.M. Didn't get my mother anything so she has been in a bad mood all morning.
1 P.M. My father said, "If I were you, lad, I'd nip round Cherry's and get your mother a card and present." He gave me two pounds so I got a card saying "Mummy I love you" (it was the only one left, just my luck), and five boxes of liquorice allsorts (going cheap because the boxes were squashed). She cheered up and didn't even mind when my father took a bunch of tulips round to grandma's and came back five hours later smelling of drink.

Pandora's mother was taken out and spoilt in a restaurant. I will do the same for my mother when I am famous.

Monday   March 22nd

I have catalogued my bedroom library. I have got a hundred and fifty-one books, not counting the Enid Blytons.

Tuesday   March 23rd

I will be fifteen in eleven days. So I have only got to wait one year and eleven days to get married, should I want to.

Wednesday   March 24th

The only thing that really worries me about my appearance now is my ears. They stick out at an angle of ninety degrees. I have checked them with my geometry set so I know it is a scientific fact.

Thursday   March 25th
LADY DAY (QUARTER DAY). NEW MOON

I have had a spiritual awakening. Two nice men representing a religious group called the Sunshine People called at the house. They talked about how they alone could bring peace to the world. It is twenty pounds to join. I will get the money somehow. Nothing is too expensive where peace is concerned.

Friday   March 26th

Tried to persuade Pandora to join the Sunshine People. She was not swayed by my arguments. They are calling round tomorrow to meet my parents and sign the agreement.

Saturday   March 27th

The Sunshine People came at six o'clock. My father made them stand on the doorstep in the rain. Their robes got wet through. My father said they were trying to brainwash a simple child. When they left my mother watched them walk up the cul-de-sac. She said, "They don't look very charismatic now, they just look bloody wet." I wept a few tears. I think I was weeping out of relief—twenty quid is a lot of money.

Sunday   March 28th
PASSION SUNDAY. BRITISH SUMMER TIME BEGINS

My father forgot to change the clocks last night so I was late for the Pink Brigade's meeting in Pandora's

lounge. We voted to exclude Pandora's father from
the meeting on the grounds of his extreme left-wing
views. We have decided to back Roy Hattersley in
the expected fight for the leadership.

Pandora has gone off Tony Benn since she found
out that he is a lapsed aristocrat.

Claire Neilson introduced a new member, her
name is Barbara Boyer. She is dead good-looking
and also dead intelligent. She disagreed with Pandora over NATO's nuclear arms policy. Pandora had
to concede that China was an unknown factor. Pandora asked Claire Neilson not to bring Barbara
again.

Monday   March 29th

I ate my school dinner sitting next to Barbara Boyer.
She is a truly wonderful girl. She pointed out that
Pandora has got a lot of faults. I was forced to agree
with her.

Tuesday   March 30th

I am committing non-sexual adultery with Barbara.
I am at the center of an eternal triangle. Nigel is the
only one to know: he has been sworn to secrecy.

Wednesday   March 31st

Nigel has blabbed it all over the school. Pandora
spent the afternoon in matron's office.

Thursday   April 1st
ALL FOOLS' DAY. MOON'S FIRST QUARTER

Barbara Boyer has ended our brief *affaire*. I rang her
up at the pet shop where she works part time cleaning the cages out. She said she couldn't bear to see
the pain in Pandora's eyes. I asked her if it was an

April Fools' joke, she said no and pointed out that it was after 12 A.M.

I have learnt an important lesson, because of lust I am without love.

I am fifteen tomorrow.

Had a shave to cheer myself up.

Friday   April 2nd

I am fifteen, but legally I am still a child. There is nothing I can do today that I couldn't do yesterday. Worse luck!

Had seven cards from relations and three from friends. My presents were the usual load of Japanese rubbish, though I did get a model airplane from Bert that was made in West Germany.

Pandora has ignored my birthday. I don't blame her. I betrayed her trust.

Boz, Baz, Daz, Maz, Kev and Melv came back from the canal and gave me the bumps. Boz gave me a tube of glue for my model airplane.

Saturday   April 3rd

8 A.M. Britain is at war with Argentina!!! Radio Four has just announced it. I am overcome with excitement. Half of me thinks it is tragic and the other half of me thinks it is dead exciting.

10 A.M. Woke my father up to tell him Argentina has invaded the Falklands. He shot out of bed because he thought the Falklands lay off the coast of Scotland. When I pointed out that they were eight thousand miles away he got back into bed and pulled the covers over his head.

4 P.M. I have just had the most humiliating experience of my life. It started when I began to assemble my model airplane. I had nearly finished it when I thought I would try an experimental sniff of glue. I put my nose to the undercarriage and sniffed for five seconds, nothing spiritual happened but my nose stuck to the plane! My father took me to Casualty to have it removed, how I endured the laughing and sniggering I don't know.

The Casualty doctor wrote "Glue Sniffer" on my outpatient's card.

I rang Pandora; she is coming round after her viola lesson. Love is the only thing that keeps me sane . . .

By the year 2000, 2 out of 3 Americans could be illiterate.

It's true.

Today, 75 million adults...about one American in three, can't read adequately. And by the year 2000, U.S. News & World Report envisions an America with a literacy rate of only 30%.

Before that America comes to be, you can stop it...by joining the fight against illiteracy today.

Call the Coalition for Literacy at toll-free **1-800-228-8813** and volunteer.

**Volunteer
Against Illiteracy.
The only degree you need
is a degree of caring.**

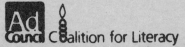

Ad Council   Coalition for Literacy

THIS AD PRODUCED BY MARTIN LITHOGRAPHERS
A MARTIN COMMUNICATIONS COMPANY

Lit 10/86